The Oaf Prince

Sienna Sway

DJINN PUBLISHING

The Oaf Prince
A Djinn book
by
Sienna Sway

Published by Djinn Publishing
www.DjinnPublishing.com

Print, 1st edition
ISBN 978-0-9949398-0-7

Cover design by: H. A. Kinani

Dedication

To me, this book will always represent a relaxed happiness. Summer stretching forever, in a time that I took off of *everything* just to write. School, work and yes, even travel, were put aside. This was the ultimate treat that I could give myself. And I can say, the time was well spent with my family, my dog and two cats, and with my mother.

During this time, I really got to know her. Not only as a mother but also as an adult, and especially, as a friend.

Although she is gone now, there is no doubt in my mind that The Oaf Prince came to be because no matter what, she always supported me.

For that reason, this book is dedicated to you, Mama, just like every other accomplishment that I might make in my life.

With love always, to Karima.

CHAPTER ONE

The ocean wind was almost a relief, buffeting at Prince Nemir's back. He hated sailing, being away from solid ground, the earth and life that it sprouted and surrounded instead by icy, unending waters. Now, after two weeks straight on the small ship with only the crew and a few of his helpers for company, he was ready to kiss the Tasnian dock, simply for being there. Nemir watched the shore approaching in the distance, his stomach twisting with the finality of it.

The only benefit that Nemir could see of this whole situation was that he would be able to see his sister, Desada. If they had planned the trip properly, he could have at least enjoyed the trip across the ocean with her.

Instead, she had been sent to strengthen the friendship between the royal families only to send a letter home after a week insisting that she was bored and wanted to come home. Add to that Nemir's "lack of direction" and disinterest in "opening himself up to the experiences the world had to offer" and it was decided that he would be sent to join her.

He scowled, remembering the long-winded lecture from his father, his mother nodding in agreement behind him. Sadly, all of his whining and reasoning did nothing to change the fact that Nemir was now arriving on the Tasnian shore.

The ship slowed and then slowed some more and then finally, it came to a stop along the harbor.

"Ready to go?"

He turned to Eliseo. His man servant stood patiently at his side, but judging by the amusement in his eyes, Nemir could tell that his apprehension was clear to see.

Without a word, Nemir nodded and began the descent from the ship.

As his boots touched the Tasnian shore for the first time, Nemir was faced with the fact that he was away from his home country for the first time. Already he was noticing little things that put him on edge—like the fact that apparently every person in this country had yellow hair of varying shades and they were all tall and broad.

Nemir stood out like a sore thumb.

The Prince was there with the royal party, unmistakable in his gaudy attire, flags held up on either side of him.

Nemir swallowed.

Even the Prince, as he marched toward Nemir purposefully and confidently, was the complete opposite of the people Nemir had shared his life with so far.

Desada had insisted that he had a dark and stormy air about him but Nemir definitely couldn't see it.

He had light brown hair at darkest, more of a gold really, and he was even paler than Nemir was. Granted, he was tall and muscular and managed to look rather foreboding—and maybe a little dashing–in his chainmail. The storminess that his little sister had described however, seemed like more of a flair for the dramatics to Nemir.

As though sensing his train of thought, Prince Allard pulled the gloves from both of his hands as he marched forward. He dropped the leather and gold to the ground as though it was worthless.

Two of his men jumped at once to retrieve them.

Nemir had a suspicion that he wasn't going to like Tasnia very much.

He raised a dark brow as Prince Allard came to a stop before him, wondering why in heaven's name the prince had decided to greet him in armor anyway?

He bowed deeply.

"I apologize for making you wait," he said, lifting his head to look up at Nemir through his soft fringe as the ocean breeze tousled it. His eyes were incredibly blue.

"There's no need, I only just—"

He cut Nemir off by taking his hand into his own and kissing it.

Spluttering, Nemir stared at the prince.

He could feel his lips moving but no sound was coming out.

"I have heard many times of the beauty of the Suvlian people, first your sister, and now you, have thoroughly convinced me."

He smiled with a look in his eye that suddenly put Nemir's body into motion again.

He yanked his hand from the other man's grasp and slapped him harder than he'd ever hit anything in his life.

His hand stung immediately and as Prince Allard stumbled back, a hand touching the side of his face in shock, his men caught him. And Nemir belatedly remembered the most important part of all this; Prince Allard, displaying unseemly behavior or not, was still a prince.

He felt his indignation draining away and with a grimace, he watched him straighten and look at Nemir with an ill-concealed fire in his eyes. Nemir had always been quick to cover his emotions with anger and irritation, but this time he may have gone too far.

"I did not realize that it was the way of your people to treat your hosts in such a manner," Prince Allard spat.

Nemir shook his head, his mind racing.

"You misunderstand me," he said hastily. "In my country we only hit those who we are *truly* appreciative of."

Prince Allard eyed him narrowly.

"You don't do that here?" Nemir rushed on, glancing around at the many people on the port.

When all of Prince Allard's help simply stared at him with wide eyes and his own companions avoided eye contact, he cleared his throat loudly and shot a threatening look at Eliseo.

"It's true," Eliseo said uncomfortably. He dusted off his jacket, avoiding eye contact.

Nemir grimaced and pushed on.

"Highness," he said, striding forward. "It's been a long journey on unkind waters. I don't suppose we could continue this conversation indoors after a long rest?"

A trained propriety instantly took the other prince over.

"Of course," he said coming forward at once and offering his arm.

Nemir swallowed and slipped his fingers into the prince's elbow without arguing. Judging by the prince's ease touching Nemir and treating him more or less like he was a woman, it was safe to assume that men here didn't see things quite the same way they did in Suvahl.

Oh well. He just hoped that the little lie would last long enough for him to have a deep and undisturbed sleep in a warm, unmoving bed.

The thought almost made his mouth water.

Following a painfully awkward carriage ride, Nemir was escorted gratefully to a bed. He barely noticed anything around him, registering only trees passing from the window and eventually cobble stones beneath the wheels until he finally sank under warm covers on blessedly still ground.

He didn't care if he never set foot on a ship again.

***

Nemir woke with a violent sneeze.

He rubbed his nose furiously and snuggled back into the covers without opening his eyes. Almost at once, his nose began to tickle again.

He rubbed at it again until he heard a soft giggle. His eyes shot open.

"Desada!" he exclaimed.

His sister launched herself into his arms, tossing aside a suspiciously long feather, her mass of dark, curly hair nearly suffocating him.

"I've missed you!" she cried. "Let's never be apart again!"

"It's only been a month," Nemir said, hiding his pleased smile.

"Yes I know," she said. "But we've never been apart for so long."

She pulled back and laid down next to him, her small pouty lips in a frown.

"And it's *dreadfully* boring here," she whispered. "The women aren't allowed to do a thing. We simply sit around and chat all day."

Nemir frowned.

"Really?" he asked. "What about?"

"Absolutely *nothing*," she moaned.

His frown deepened. That seemed counterproductive, but from what he'd heard, Tasnia's culture was difficult for all but the locals to comprehend.

"Well don't worry," he said. "While I'm here, you won't be so bored at least."

"It's already better," she said, grinning impishly. "Especially since you've already started a commotion."

Nemir sat up.

"What commotion? I've only just arrived."

"Yes, and slapped the heir to the thrown already?" she asked.

He groaned.

"You heard about that?" he asked. "How?"

"I'm a lady," she said simply. "Here in Tasnia, the ladies have a way of knowing everything."

She bounced out of bed and pulled out a chair at the breakfast table and sat down.

"It's better known as *gossip*," she said, popping a strawberry into her mouth. "And Prince Allard seems to be the main source of it."

"Are they very angry?" Nemir asked.

"I don't think so, but everyone is shocked. No one goes against Prince Allard."

With a sigh, Nemir pulled himself grudgingly out of bed and sat down across from his sister.

She wrinkled her nose at his appearance and he shrugged.

"I was too tired to change," he said. Although right now the smell emanating from him seemed like more of an issue than his clothes. He tried not to breathe out of his nose and examined the food on the table.

The strawberries were about the only thing he recognized. There was a bowl of them accompanied by another of some sort of cream, and a small silver platter. Nemir lifted the lid, uncovering what looked like thin sheets of batter, loosely rolled and topped with more fruit and cream.

He frowned at the meal and lifted a small forkful to taste it. After nearly choking at the sweetness, he swallowed the food down with a long gulp of water.

He glanced up at Desada and found her giggling again.

"It does take some getting used to," she admitted, grabbing the fork out of his hand and cutting off a generous portion of the desert.

"I like it," she said, shoving the whole piece into her mouth.

"But dessert for breakfast?"

She shrugged and then fixed her gaze passed Nemir, her eyes wide.

"Eliseo!" she squealed and promptly choked on all the food in her mouth.

Nemir's tall and lanky caretaker slipped into the lavish bedchamber, coming to pat Desada on the back until her gasping subsided.

She looked up at Eliseo through teary eyes.

"Eliseo," she said. "Has it been so long? Your mustache has turned all grey."

He smiled softly.

"My mustache has been grey since you were a child," he said, shaking his head.

He glanced at the untouched meal and nodded.

"I'll have to speak to the palace chef," he said simply. He ran his eyes over Nemir's disheveled form with an ill-disguised grimace. "But first, I think it's best if I arrange for a bath."

Desada snorted into her drink in a very un-lady-like manner.

Nemir scowled.

***

The bathing chamber was large, brightened by a roof made entirely of glass, the light then reflected with walls of mirrors.

Nemir almost felt like he was outside. Everywhere he turned, he saw sunshine, blue skies, fluffy clouds—and the help and himself of course, but he was trying to ignore that part of it.

He had lost some weight during the long journey across the Capri Sea, and his hair, normally as shiny and curly as his sister's lay dull and limp across his skin. He looked tired, his softly tanned skin now sallow with bags under his eyes. To top it all off, he had a shadow of blotchy, dark grey across his chin. He didn't need to shave often, but when he left it too long, the hair never grew in thickly or evenly.

Feeling like an utter disgrace for showing himself to royalty like this, he pulled at the strings on his shirt and several hands were suddenly helping him.

His cheeks began to burn as he belatedly remembered how many people were still in the room with him. He brushed the other boy's hands away and tugged his shirt tightly closed against himself.

"I don't need help bathing," he said with a nervous laugh.

They seemed rather confused by that but Nemir didn't budge until every one of the boys had left the room, shutting the door securely behind them.

Most places had help reserved for tasks like these, but Nemir didn't like it. He never had and as soon as he'd become old enough to realize that he appreciated a little privacy, he had insisted on bathing and dressing alone.

Satisfied that he was now on his own, he pulled his clothes from his tired body. Dipping his toe into the warm water to test the temperature. He then sank down gratefully into the heat.

He sighed and shut his eyes, half hoping that he could stay here all day.

That was another thing that he truly appreciated—not having to socialize with new people...

No doubt the day would be filled with meeting dignitaries, King Jareth and his wife Queen Barnett, being two of them.

His stomach squirmed at the thought and he sank into the water until his whole head was submerged. Sure, he spent his entire life with royalty, but his mother and father hardly counted.

Only when he began to shiver from the cold water, did Nemir grudgingly pull himself from the bath.

He wrapped himself in the long white robe provided and found Eliseo waiting in his chambers with a fresh and rather elaborate outfit for him. It seemed that he would be lavished in rich burgundy velvet, and gold ornamentation. Cream and ivory poked out from the pile and Nemir ran his hands over the mass.

He was sure he hadn't packed anything like these.

"What's all this?" he asked.

"It's Tasnian formal wear," Eliseo said as Nemir lifted a long gold chain from the pile.

Eliseo pulled the string of metal from his fingers and replaced it with a razor and shaving cream.

"Let's get you more presentable before you are put before the King and Queen."

Nemir took a seat a little nervously. He had to shave so rarely that he still found the act embarrassingly frightening.

Eliseo prepared everything promptly, wetting his face and applying the cream, covering his chest with a towel. Only when the long silver blade was brought to his skin did Nemir squeeze his eyes shut and try not to move.

"You have nothing to be nervous about," Eliseo assured him. "It's just going to be a simple dinner, from what I was told. There will be only a few guests and you will sit with your sister by the royal family so that you can get to know one another a little bit more. The whole point of this is to create a strong bond between your families, after all."

Nemir swallowed, Eliseo's words adding to his frazzled nerves.

He wasn't very good at getting to know people.

***

Nemir tried in vain to keep his eyes in his head, but it was difficult when everywhere he glanced, some unknown object was shining at him.

The Tasnian clothes alone were so heavily ornamented by silver and gold and glass hanging from all directions, that Nemir could scarcely remember the faces of all the dinner guests seated around him.

"You're going to make me blush if you continue to stare like that."

Nemir looked up from the jewels on the decorated white suit he was staring at and realized that he'd been looking at Prince Allard.

He blushed at the look the blond was giving him and quickly looked away. It was impossible not to note that there was an annoyed glint in his eyes. Apparently, the subject of the slap had not been forgotten.

Nemir swallowed and attempted to eat some more of the meat which seemed to have been drowned in honey and oranges.

"So Nemir, how do you like what you've seen of Tasnia so far?"

Nemir looked at the King, who was only a seat away at the head of the table and the most decorated of all the dinner guests. He was the complete opposite of his son in nature. They looked much the same but where Allard tried to be impressive, the king was actually intimidating.

At his words, the table quieted and everyone waited for his answer, curiously.

He swallowed down his mouthful, nearly choking on the syrup and cleared his throat.

"Well, I—I haven't really seen any—any of the country yet," he stuttered.

Why did he stutter?

He saw Desada smirk from the corner of his eye and silently cursed her. It wasn't his fault that he did that under pressure.

"Just this lovely palace," he amended.

"Hm. Well in a week's time we were planning to accompany you and your lovely sister to the capitol. There will be the summer solstice celebration and parade. It really is fortunate that you arrived today. Shortly after the parade, the summer theatre festival will launch. People come from across the land to watch our performers," he said proudly, and then frowned. "You will need something to do in the meantime, I suppose."

"I don't mind spending my time here," Nemir stammered but King Jareth was exchanging a thoughtful glance with his wife.

"Well, that won't do at all, will it?" she asked.

She reached over and placed a hand on her son's arm.

"Why don't you take Nemir and Desada on a small tour tomorrow?"

A frown flittered across Allard's face but he covered it quickly with a charming smile.

"I'm afraid I was planning to go hunting tomorrow," he said easily. "A two day trip."

His father frowned.

"Go the next day," he said. "You will take them to the capitol and then the farming villages north of the city."

This time, Allard's ill-concealed frown was more obvious.

"But the princess has already seen those places and I already have all of my hunting gear ready to go."

Nemir shifted awkwardly.

"It's okay," he said.

The king shook his head sternly, making Nemir sink back into his seat.

"You are our guests. We want you to enjoy your stay here."

He glanced at his son and sighed.

"Show them around after you come back then," he suggested, and this time Allard smiled a little smugly and didn't argue it.

Nemir tried not to glare. He didn't particularly *want* to have a tour with the prince but seeing proof that Allard always got his way, explained his lacking personality.

"And why don't you take Nemir hunting with you tomorrow?" his mother added sweetly.

Nemir's eyes widened and he looked at Allard. There were several problems with the queen's suggestion, the first of which being that Nemir had no interest or ability to kill or track any animals. At all. The second of which being that Prince Allard was particularly difficult to endure and now he would have to spend two whole days with him?

Clearly, Prince Allard was thinking similar things, as he did not answer and only stared at his mother in agitation.

"Normally, I hunt alone," he finally said through clenched teeth.

"Then you won't mind some extra company," King Jareth said at once.

At his father's warning tone, Allard grimaced and nodded.

He shot Nemir a haughty glare.

"I hope that you're a swift hunter," he said. "I don't appreciate being slowed down."

"Nonsense," the queen said. "All boys know how to hunt."

Nemir grimaced.

"He won't slow you down." Desada suddenly piped up. "He's an excellent hunter."

"Really?" Allard asked, looking instantly relieved.

Nemir stared at his disloyal sister, attempting not to let his jaw drop.

"Oh yes," she continued, shooting him an amused look. "The only things that might deter him are Oves."

A thrill of foreboding ran down Nemir's spine.

"What are Oves?" he asked uneasily.

"They're ogre hybrids," Prince Allard said easily.

Nemir's blood ran cold.

"*Ogres*?" he demanded. "You have *ogres* in this land?"

He'd heard of other, terrifying, creatures in the Tasnian wilds, but ogres had never been mentioned, until now.

"Yes," Desada answered at once. The little wench was enjoying this far too much. "And they haven't been very happy with the royal family lately."

She smiled sympathetically.

"Have fun on your hunting trip dear brother," she said.

If Nemir thought that he had a chance to beat his little sister in a duel, this would definitely be the moment that he challenged her to one.

Instead, he just sat in silence while the royal family tried unsuccessfully to ease his quivering nerves.

CHAPTER TWO

"We've told you a hundred times that the ogres won't come near you," Eliseo said patiently. "You probably won't even catch a glimpse of any of them."

"They're ogres, Nemir! Do you honestly expect them to organize an attack?!"

Nemir turned to his sister who began to giggle at once at his scowl.

"This is *your* fault!" he shouted.

She erupted into a fit of snorting laughter, rolling around on his bed.

"You know very well that I can barely hold a bow, let alone shoot one!"

Her ridiculous snorting and gasping didn't even make him smile. Instead, he marched over to the bed and caught his sister's arm as she beat one of his pillows into oblivion through her laughter.

"Get out," he said, pulling her.

"What?" she asked, looking up at him through her tears.

"Out!"

He tugged her to the door and shoved her through it, slamming it shut in her face. Nemir didn't regret it when he heard her hysterical laughter continue from the hallway.

He walked over to the vanity and sat down in a slump, looking at himself in the mirror. Nemir preferred gardening to hunting and singing to sword point.

Desada was the true 'son' in the family, that much was clear to everyone in Suvahl, but here in Tasnia, they seemed to be stuck on the idea of women in skirts and men on horses.

Horseback riding made his thighs hurt.

He sighed heavily as Eliseo came up behind him, binding his nearly shoulder length hair back with a thin leather strap.

"Don't worry," he said, placing a hand on his shoulder. "You've hunted before. You're not completely useless."

He smiled at Nemir in his calming way, the edges of his moustache pointing up on either side.

Nemir sighed. Yes and on those occasions, he had been forced to accept his fate. One more time wouldn't hurt.

***

The summer sun shone down on their leave of the palace grounds. Nemir was surprised by the lack of ceremony. In Suvahl, no hunting party left from the palace without some sort of farewell.

He could only assume that Prince Allard rode off into the wild often enough that no one cared anymore.

The prince nodded at him and kicked his lovely mare ahead, assuming that Nemir would ride along after him.

It had been sometime since he had been on the back of a horse, but of course he knew how to ride fairly well.

The silver speckled stallion jerked a little, under his unpracticed legs but as he eased into riding again, he trotted up next to Allard on the path.

"So what will we be hunting for?" he asked.

Allard glanced over at him.

"I like to hunt Elk," he said easily. "They're big, and it's much more impressive when you drag one home."

"Ah, of course," Nemir said.

What was an elk?

The silence dragged on as they rode down the path, watching the forest grow larger and larger in the distance, until finally, they entered it.

His legs were beginning to seize up and clench already.

"How much farther will we go?" he asked.

Allard raised a brow.

"Until we find an animal we'd like to shoot."

He glanced down at Nemir's awkward shifting.

"Are you done already?" he asked.

Nemir tried not to blush. He forced himself to sit still.

"I have been on a ship for the past week," he said defensively. "My legs are not use to this anymore."

Not to mention that his back was already killing him.

Allard frowned.

"We'll head back before the evening then," he said.

Grateful, Nemir sat up straight and focused on keeping up with the prince.

It had been so long since Nemir had been in a proper forest that the unfamiliar sights and sounds, under other circumstances, would have been peaceful and fascinating. After another hour on horseback however, his internal debate of whether or not to give up and simply ride back to the palace, kept him from noticing anything beyond his screaming muscles.

Was he really this out of shape?

His right thigh began to jerk spasmodically and finally, he jerked his horse to a stop.

"Prince Allard," he said, smacking at his leg until the muscle lay still. "I need a rest."

The blond prince raised a brow, but climbed off of his horse without a word.

He watched Nemir as he struggled to climb down with his stiff muscles and finally, with an amused smile, he came to help him.

"I take it that you're not quite the hunter that your sister described you to be."

Nemir sighed.

"Not at all," he admitted with a grimace. "She enjoys watching me humiliate myself."

"How charming," Allard said.

He watched Nemir as he stretched out, his back and shoulders cracking loudly.

"We're in the vicinity where I often find the deer and elk," Allard said. "If you'd like, we can continue on foot for a while."

Nemir looked at the prince. He didn't seem to mind, but Nemir knew he was truly ruining the sport for him.

"There's no need," he said. "You can go on ahead on your horse. I don't mind waiting."

The prince stared at him for a moment and then slapped Nemir so hard across the face that he stumbled and nearly fell.

Shocked, Nemir looked up at Allard, holding his stinging cheek.

"What's the matter?" Allard asked innocently. "I just wanted to show you how much I appreciate your offer."

Nemir stared at him, stunned, until the corners of prince Allard's lips tilted and he broke into a grin.

Despite himself, Nemir laughed.

"Now we're even."

Allard laughed and smacked him companionably on the back.

"Now forget about all that waiting business, will you?" He dropped an arm around Nemir's shoulders. "We are here to hunt, and that's what we shall do."

He tossed him an apple from one of their packs and led him along. Walking was such a relief that Nemir was tempted to kiss Allard—or more like, not be offended if Allard tried to kiss *him* again.

"Try to keep quiet," Allard whispered. "We don't have much time if we want to be home before dark."

They were leaving the trail now, and everything was quieter and louder at the same time. The air felt so still and thick that every noise was magnified tenfold by the silence.

Nemir realized how loudly his leather boots were crunching into the soft forest floor and tried to lighten his step. He looked at Allard's feet, trying to mimic the way that he walked, rolling from the heel to the ball of his foot.

It helped a little, but he was still fairly sure that the horses were quieter than he was.

For some time, they crept in silence, until Nemir's thighs began to ache again.

Really, how long had he been this out of shape for?

He thought back to the gardens and the sanctuary back home wistfully, remembering how much time he'd opted to spend there before he was sent to this forsaken land.

Okay, maybe 'forsaken land' was a bit harsh, but it was different and that was bad enough.

He sighed heavily.

Allard shot him a look and he sighed again—more quietly of course.

Suddenly, Allard stilled, his eyes glued ahead of him.

Nemir crept forward, trying to see what Allard was staring so intently at.

He caught a glimpse of soft brown fur and for a moment he thought that it was a horse, but no, it was too big. And then he saw the antlers— large and reaching.

He gasped.

"What's that?" he squeaked.

The creature started, looked straight at them, and then leaped off at break-neck speed.

Nemir stared after it, his mouth hanging open.

"That was amazing!" he exclaimed.

He looked at Allard, the grin slipping off of his face.

"That was an elk," Allard said simply.

"Ah."

Nemir cleared his throat awkwardly.

"We could—follow it," he suggested.

Allard sighed loudly and pushed himself up from his crouched position.

"Is there a point?" he asked.

He dusted off his pants.

"Let's just head back."

Nemir tried not to look too excited by the suggestion. He dropped into step next to Allard, offering him a hesitant smile.

Truth be told, he had never been on a successful hunt before, nor did he really care to be on one. He much preferred controlled environments to the wild, and relaxation to adrenaline rushes.

They reached their horses much faster than Nemir expected to and probably only because they were putting so much less care into keeping quiet.

Nemir practically ran to the stallion in relief. At the last moment, his foot caught on a stray branch, sending him sprawling across the path.

He spat out dirt while Allard stood back, laughing loudly. He didn't bother trying to hide it, but he at least had the decency to help Nemir back up to his feet.

"So tell me something," Allard started as they began their trek back up the path, this time on their mounts. "How often do you go hunting back home?"

Nemir laughed.

"I don't," he said.

"Why am I not surprised?" Allard muttered.

Nemir couldn't help but laugh. This was nothing compared to his previous hunting escapades.

"The last time I went was more than three years ago. My father wanted me to go," he said. "After that, the royal hunting party made a personal request to my father that I not be forced to join them again."

The other prince howled with laughter.

"The whole hunting party?" he asked.

Nemir nodded, still smiling.

It was more of a joke than anything. In fact, Nemir had been the one to suggest the idea.

His father hadn't listened to him for years, especially when it came to sports, but he couldn't ignore so many of his own friends when they begged him so fervently.

"It was for the common good," Nemir said solemnly.

They were both still smiling when they emerged from the thinning trees around them.

Nemir blinked away from the evening sun which blazed down on them in a deep orange. He turned his face from it, finding that Allard had stopped. He was staring ahead, a guarded expression on his face.

Nemir followed his gaze, finding the sun striking several figures in the distance.

At a first glance they appeared to be normal, they seemed human, but even from this distance, their size could not be ignored.

A soft chill ran down his spine.

The men and women alike, wore only what looked like tattered rags of what once *might* have been clothing, draped over their exposed bodies, hiding only the most important parts. Strange piercings adorned their muscular, tanned bodies. They all had long hair of varying, vibrant colors, tied up in intricate knots that hung all the way to their hips nonetheless.

The group of them as one, seemed to sense the presence of the two princes. Together, they all turned and faced the boys.

None of them moved; their bright eyes fixed on the two in silence.

"Let's go," Allard whispered.

He nudged his horse into motion, Nemir close at his side.

In complete silence, they rode past the group. Nemir couldn't help but glance at them as they did. They were all still watching. The silence was more unnerving than even their intent, narrow eyes and the bones pierced through their flesh, glinting white in the sun.

As the group finally fell into the distance and out of sight, Nemir inhaled a deep breath, realizing he had been holding it the entire time.

"They don't usually come this close to the palace, or the cities," Allard said.

"Is that so?" Nemir asked. Then why were they here? His stomach was still twisting anxiously. Until they were on the palace grounds again, he doubted that it would stop.

They didn't look quite as hideous as Nemir had expected them to look, but they were even more intimidating, if that was possible.

"Can we hurry?" he asked.

Allard glanced at him and began to nod but as he did, his eyes drifted over Nemir's shoulder, his jaw slackening. He whipped out his sword and before Nemir knew what was happening, they were surrounded.

His heart ricocheted into his ribs as his eyes locked with the large ogre before him. He looked almost straight into the large green eyes, despite the fact that he was on horseback and the other was on foot. The monster grinned down at him, displaying a set of pearly white teeth and Nemir was positive that he would die from fright.

Suddenly, he was struck across the back of his head. As his face drew near to the grassy earth, everything went black.

CHAPTER THREE

Soluc grimaced at the blood dripping thickly down his biceps. The wolf bone had been ripped straight from its piercing at the tip of his shoulder by his own carelessness. He supposed that it made him look that much more intimidating, but the stinging pain was rather unwelcome when he had so much on his mind.

"Where is my brother?" he demanded harshly. He kicked the wooden beam of said brother's tent in emphasis, sending the whole structure crumpling to the ground.

The youngsters he'd been left with, stared up at him. None of them cowered, but they eyed Soluc's impressive form like he was born from the dimmest of ogres.

"Lenroy? He's catching the prince," one said slowly.

Soluc smiled at the young oaf. He was perhaps too young to be a part of the oves militia—or as most others called it—gang. He gripped him by the elaborate stone necklace that draped around his neck and lifted the boy, with one arm, off of his feet.

The boy struggled against his grasp, smearing Soluc's blood across his neck. Soluc smiled at the anger in his young eyes and ducked easily aside from a sloppy punch, which only brushed his auburn hair.

It was better to teach him now.

"When you grow, perhaps you'll have a chance of over powering me." He tossed the youth carelessly into the midst of the others who were staring in fascination. Several of them fell in a clutter as he landed on them.

"Until then, you keep in your place."

Some of his frustration abated, Soluc turned to catch Ilaj grinning at the scene, baring a set of sharp, spiked teeth.

Soluc rolled his eyes as he came into step next to his friend.

"I love to watch you lord over people," he laughed.

"I know," Soluc said. "You told me that twice today, already."

"Only because it's true," Ilaj grinned.

Soluc suspected that it was. The Raven haired oaf enjoyed nothing more than elaborately styling his knee length hair and watching people squirm in agony. But either way, Soluc was not behaving like the animal that he was, for Ilaj's amusement.

"Buttering me up won't change the fact that Lenroy left with the team yesterday and they *still* aren't back. Not with the prince. Not with food. Not at all."

Saying it made his blood begin to boil.

"Tuboy!" His voice echoed beyond the scope of their camp and through the trees around them. A few people glanced at him with that look he'd been seeing a lot lately, but no one so much as stirred.

Soluc frowned and glanced at Ilaj, finding him grinning that annoying grin again.

"What?" he demanded.

"Tuboy went on the hunt this morning, remember?" he asked.

Soluc scowled. *Now* he did.

"Memet!" he shouted instead.

There was a moment's silence. He glanced at Ilaj about to ask him if Memet had gone too, but his other little brother poked a head out from a nearby tent.

"What?" he asked easily.

"Are you ready for a hunt?" he asked.

Memet raised a red brow.

"Didn't the hunt leave already?" he asked.

Soluc glowered at that damn expression. If one more person looked at him like he had no wisps of brain in his skull, he would personally beat them until they were too slow to judge.

"Not for food," he growled.

"Ah."

Memet climbed out of the tent fully, so that he could face his brother. He was undressed, his long muscular form covered only by the hip length hair that was left open and draped over his body.

"More piercings?" Soluc asked, noticing the small clamp that was still attached to the skin on his collar.

"Just a few," he said with a shrug. "So are you going to tell me what we're hunting, or do I have to force it from you?"

"Force it from him," Ilaj encouraged. "There hasn't been a decent brawl in weeks."

Memet smiled, but waited while Soluc shot his friend a scathing look.

"Yes, and what a shame that we have no one too injured to carry on their duties."

Ilaj chuckled.

Shaking his head, Soluc turned back to his brother, who was waiting quite patiently for an answer.

"We are going to track the hunting team that was sent to retrieve the prince," he said. "They're taking too long."

A smile touched Memet's lips.

"That should be fun," he said. "And what do we get to do them, if we find them lazing about in the forest somewhere?"

Soluc grinned. He had a wonderful brother.

"I'll tie them up, and you do whatever you like."

The glint in Memet's eyes showed Soluc his consent.

"Ilaj," he said turning to his friend. "You stay behind and let the hunting party know the deal. You'll be the eldest here, so keep charge."

"Of course," Ilaj murmured.

Suddenly, Memet tilted his head, his eyes narrowed.

"Hm," he muttered with a frown. "It doesn't look like we'll be going after all."

"What?"

He tilted his head, attempting to make out whatever noise his keen brother was hearing.

"The prince-hunting team is arriving," Memet said.

Soluc's heart careened into his chest with nerves. Had they caught the Tasnian prince? More importantly, was he still alive?

"Let me finish this," Memet said, indicating the clamp still squeezing his skin, "and I'll join you to greet them."

"Let me do it for you," Ilaj said at once.

Memet shrugged and re-entered the tent, Ilaj close behind him.

His heart continuing to thunder in his chest, Soluc paced to the edge of the camp ground wondering which way they'd come from.

They had gone west toward the human towns, the capitol and the palace, but knowing his brother, they could return from any direction.

And of course, there was a loud ruckus, laughter and cheering on the *opposite* end of the camp.

With a sigh, Soluc rushed to the east of the camp, not needing to shove the crowd of young soldiers from his path, when the hunters did it themselves.

Soluc watched as two of the oves carried a bundle to the front and dropped it unceremoniously at his feet.

Without moving, Soluc waited for his brother Lenroy to escape from the applauding mix of people and approach his older brother with an unabashed grin and a glint in his green eyes.

"Is he still alive?" Soluc asked.

"Beats me," Lenroy said.

The jovial laughter had Soluc grimacing.

"Check him," he muttered to Memet, who had just arrived on the scene, newly dressed and with a line of thin bone piercing his flesh in an intricate design like the pendant from a necklace.

He bent down at once, releasing the edges of the rough fabric from the motionless form and exposing the young human prince. His head hung at an awkward angle, exposing a smooth expanse of skin on his neck, but his dark hair hid his face, and what seemed like a ridiculous amount of clothing, hid the rest of him. Everyone was silent in fascination. This was the first time many of them had ever been so close to a human.

It was Soluc's first time as well, and he wondered curiously why Prince Allard's hair was so short. Were humans always this small? He had heard that they were, but to see it from such closeness… He looked so delicate. Had they hit him too hard?

He held his breath as Memet leaned a pointed ear to the human's mouth.

After a painfully long moment, he looked up with a smile.

"He's alive."

The whole camp erupted into cheers.

"And the message?" Soluc asked, clapping Lenroy warmly on the back. "You sent it off?" he asked.

"No need to," Lenroy answered proudly. "There was another human with him. We sent the thing howling to the castle."

Soluc's smile faltered uneasily.

He whistled loudly and after a tense moment, Shaw circled the air above him with a cry and swooped down to grace Soluc's arm, her claws drawing blood, like they often did.

He stroked the hawk's beak softly.

"Did you have fun with my brother?" he asked.

He smiled as she nipped him affectionately.

"Well, if the message wasn't clear enough, we'll just send him another."

With the arrival of the human prince, the camp suddenly had the air of a party. Soluc grinned at all the happy faces.

"Prepare for a feast!" he shouted. Cheering erupted. "And if the hunting team has come up short for the night, we'll eat one of *them*!"

The laughter was contagious. Soluc turned to head back to his tent and without a word Memet bent and lifted the prince, fabric and all, from the muddy ground and followed Soluc.

He placed the prince with surprising gentleness onto Soluc's sleeping mat and looked up at him.

"We should probably make sure he'll survive," Memet said. "If he *is* going to die before our ransom is met, then we may as well prepare for battle now."

Soluc grimaced.

His brother was right. They couldn't mess up where it concerned the humans and their prince; the outcome would be too unpleasant.

He bent down next to Memet and pulled back the fabric gently.

"Check his head for bumps or cuts," Memet said.

Doing as he was told, Soluc stroked prince Allard's hair back, examining his face first. For such a small being, he had strong features; a straight nose, square jaw, high cheekbones, but his skin was just too soft.

Soluc ran his fingertips over his cheeks and neck, feeling it again.

Skin like this did not belong on an adult, he decided.

He looked up at a ripping noise and found Memet tearing the front of the prince's shirt open to examine his chest.

Soluc raised a brow. Okay, maybe he *was* a grown man, despite his small size and smooth skin. Chests like that did not belong on children. He was slight but defined.

Shaking his head, Soluc went back to his task, running his fingers deep into the thick, dark hair.

"There's a bump on the back of his skull, here," he said, "and one at the front, here."

Memet came to examine the spots indicated and finally, sat back with a sigh.

"No cuts, a few bruises and two small lumps."

He looked up at Soluc with an amused smile.

"Hard to believe, but it looks like they did a good job."

Soluc grinned.

"Yeah," he agreed. "I definitely did not expect that."

Suddenly the good-natured noise from outside magnified and Memet stood up at once.

"The hunting team is back," he said. "I'm going to go to Tuboy."

Soluc nodded, letting him go to his twin and hoping that they had managed to catch big game for the night.

A soft moan drew Soluc's attention back to the form in front of him. He crouched down even lower to look at the human as he began to sigh and shift in discomfort.

Prince Allard moaned again and it became clear that it was a moan of pain.

Slowly, his eyes fluttered open, focusing on the canopy above them for a moment before he shut them tightly again and pressed a hand to the back of his head.

Soluc smiled.

The little thing *was* delicate it would seem, or a little bump on the head wouldn't have been enough to knock him out cold for hours.

Finally, his eyes fluttered open again, exposing dark eyes of a depth that Soluc had never seen before.

He stared at the color — almost black, he was sure — with wonder until they focused on him.

The prince blinked at Soluc blankly, until Soluc thought to say something. He wasn't very good at kidnapping people, it would seem.

"Hello, Prince Allard," he said softly. His father had once said that being gentle was the best way to deal with humans. "Don't be alarmed. You won't be harmed as long as your family answers our ransom."

Said prince, furrowed his brow in confusion and then shut his eyes with another hiss of pain.

When he opened them again, the focus was slipping even farther from his eyes.

"I'm not Prince Allard," he said.

Soluc had misheard him.

He leaned in.

"What?" he asked. His voice came out unnecessarily sharp but the prince didn't seem to notice.

"I'm Nemir," he murmured. "From Suvahl."

And he was out.

Soluc sat in silence for a long moment, the blood rushing so swiftly through his ears that he couldn't hear himself think.

One name climbed to the surface of his mind.

"Lenroy!" he shouted.

CHAPTER FOUR

Nemir climbed from the dredges of sleep, relief swamping him with the knowledge that he must have been dreaming.

He squeezed his eyes shut against the light, grimacing at the throbbing pain in his head.

He'd dreamed he was attacked by ogres. The thought was so ridiculous that he must have imagined it. In fact, his short stay at the Tasnian palace seemed far too surreal to have actually happened. He must still be on the ship.

Everything felt like it was spinning.

Nemir took a deep breath to calm his stomach and tasted smoke. Something was wrong.

Something was *very* wrong.

Bright green eyes peered down at him curiously in his memory and he jerked his head up so quickly that he smacked it into the beam of wood behind him.

Gasping, he opened his eyes, sound suddenly rushing his ears like he had been submerged in water and was now breaking the surface.

The first things he heard were drums and laughter, loud and raucous. The first thing he saw was fire.

He jerked again, so hard that the ropes binding him dug painfully into his arms and shoulders.

He was tied, sitting upright.

Everything hurt.

"He's awake!" said a loud, booming voice.

All tremors of dread which had been shouting at Nemir to *not look,* were pushed aside by the man's words. He looked to his right.

Enormous men and women sat nearly naked, leering at him in the flickering light of the bonfire, their sharply pointed ears catching the light like horns. Another bonfire behind them was decorated by what looked like a full deer roasting above it and more ogres seated around it. Makeshift tents were erected behind them.

He looked to the left and found much the same sight.

The world began to swim again.

He was surrounded.

"He's scared!" one of them laughed. Nemir wished he could do *worse* than slap her, but first of all, he valued his life and second of all, he was shaking so hard he thought that he might vomit.

"Wh—why am I here?" he demanded.

Dammit, his voice was trembling.

Someone stood up from the large circle and came toward Nemir, hushing the crowd around the fire.

As he drew up to Nemir, his height—taller than any man Nemir had ever seen, seemed to stretch on until he was towering over him.

Nemir watched him in the growing silence, wondering what the giant ogre would do. Only one thing seemed logical.

"Are you going to eat me?" he asked in a small voice.

The entire camp burst into wild laughter that went on for far too long.

Finally, the one standing over him knelt down, still chuckling.

Nemir was startled to realize that he almost recognized the brute's face—his bright green eyes were so similar to the ones belonging to his captor, but this oaf was even more frightening.

"We're not going to eat you," he said, but the smile still on his face and the glint of the fire light did little to relieve that suspicion.

Nemir tried to look away, but found his eyes landing on a gash across the ogre's shoulder. He followed the trail of dried blood down his arm and felt again, like he might puke.

He shut his eyes, fighting for his train of thought.

"Why d—did you bring me here?" he demanded.

When he opened his eyes again, the giant was directing a harsh glare elsewhere.

Nemir followed his gaze despite himself, his eyes landing on a familiar face. His blood suddenly ran cold. He had seen that face grinning at him the moment before everything disappeared and he'd awoken here… although, the black eye gracing the ogre's face was new.

"It was a mistake," the ogre before him finally said.

The harsh tone of his voice sent a shiver through Nemir. He flinched when the ogre turned his gaze back to him, although his expression was surprisingly unthreatening.

"We meant to grab your friend, but it seems he *escaped*."

A loud snickering ensued at this and Nemir glanced at the ogre who had captured him, finding him shooting glares in all directions at the sound.

"If you can help us get Prince Allard, then you have nothing to worry about."

He said it as though it was nothing, with what Nemir assumed was supposed to be a charming smile, but it made him feel even more frightened.

"I can't," Nemir said.

The ogre frowned as the snickering turned into muttering.

"Why not?" he asked, the coldness in his tone, now directed at Nemir.

Nemir stifled a shiver.

"I don't know anything about Prince Allard," he said firmly. "We've only met briefly."

There was one thing Nemir knew; no matter what kind of a person Allard was, he was not about to sacrifice him to a bunch of blood hungry ogres.

The head ogre stared at him for a long moment.

"Just kill him, then!" someone shouted.

The cheer that followed was so deafening that the hair rose on the back of Nemir's neck. He half expected the leader to defend him, but he didn't look interested. He looked angry.

He shot a hot look to Nemir's black eyed kidnapper and Nemir realized that the anger wasn't aimed at him.

"Very well then," he said, pushing to his feet. "How shall we dispose of him?"

Nemir's heart dropped. He'd almost forgotten that they were monsters. What else would they keep him for?

"Burn him!"

"Let's pull him apart limb by limb!"

No. His vision was swimming.

"Let's hunt him like game!"

He couldn't die yet.

"Let me have my way with him first!"

Shocked, raucous laughter.

They couldn't kill him.

He looked up, all of the figures waving like they were caught in the heat of the flames.

"You would really destroy the whole of Tasnia for a little fun with *me*?" he demanded. Funny, now his voice sounded so strong.

The head ogre looked at him narrowly.

"What do you mean?" he asked. "You just said that you're not a prince, what difference will your death make?"

Nemir's eyes widened.

"*Prince Allard!* I said that I am not *Prince Allard!* I'm the crown prince of Suvahl, and if you have any wish to preserve the life of your species, you will *not* touch a hair on my head or my father will have your carcasses on his dinner table!"

His voice rang out hoarsely into the sudden silence.

The head ogre bent down and seized Nemir's chin, forcing him to look up into his frighteningly intense eyes.

"Is that true?" he demanded in a quiet, resonating voice.

Nemir nodded.

And threw up.

The watery mass just missed the ogre's face, striking his shoulder and his hair, before Nemir was bent over as far as the ropes would allow him to be, emptying the rest of his stomach.

When he lifted his head again, everyone was laughing.

With a grimace, the ogre wiped his shoulder and rung out his hand, splashing several of the ogres sitting nearby.

"Tuboy, Memet," he called. "Take him to your tent."

His voice was growing more distant.

Two lean and young looking oves with fiery red hair emerged from the crowds; their identical faces neared Nemir as everything began to swim in darkness.

"No one touches him," was the last thing that he heard.

***

"Soluc should count his luck."

"I guess."

Nemir lay very still as awareness dawned on him. He was laying down on something hard and cold, his arms were strained behind his back. He could feel the bindings cutting into his skin and wondered how long they'd been cutting off his circulation.

More importantly, there were two— possibly more people with him, wherever he was.

Something silky brushed his face and one of them chuckled close to him.

"You can open your eyes," said the soft voice. "We know you're awake."

Grimacing, Nemir opened his eyes narrowly, finding the ogre leaning over him, his hair hanging all the way onto Nemir's face.

Nemir blew it away and attempted to glare up at the large creature.

A smile touched the ogre's lips.

"Hey Tuboy," he said. "Come look at this."

Another head dipped into Nemir's line of vision and then crouched down lower, staring.

For a moment Nemir thought he was seeing double until he noticed the lack of piercings adorning Tuboy's eyebrows and mouth.

"Hm," Tuboy said with a frown.

The other reached down. Nemir flinched hard, but the ogre simply brushed his hair away from his ears.

"They're so small," Tuboy said. "I wonder how he hears with them."

"I can hear just fine," Nemir said roughly.

As though just becoming aware of him, their eyes widened and with a quick glance at one another, they both chuckled.

They leaned away from him while he struggled into a sitting position and before Nemir could say another word, a bowl filled with scraps of meat was held under his nose by a large hand.

Nemir looked at it. He badly wanted to say that it looked disgusting but he doubted that his words would be heard over the sound of his stomach growling.

He swallowed and looked up at his captors indignantly.

"How am I supposed to eat this?" he asked.

After a moment of confused silence, Tuboy glanced at his brother.

"Memet," he said. "His hands."

"Right."

Memet reached around Nemir, easily freeing him from his bindings.

He stretched his fingers out at once and convulsed at the pain that surged through them as his blood returned.

He gasped, squeezing his hands to his chest, until finally the pain subsided.

"His bindings need to be tied more loosely," Memet was saying, "Or his hands might fall off."

Nemir swallowed.

He flexed his arms one more time and then silently reached for the bowl.

He didn't think he'd ever been hungrier. All of his life food had always been close at hand. Not just any food, either, gourmet delicacies of all kinds. Even Tasnia's syrupy sweet meals were made by the finest chefs, but this... Nemir was quite sure that it was the tastiest thing he'd ever eaten.

As he reached the bottom of the bowl, he realized that he was being closely watched.

He looked up at the two. Somehow, they were slightly less intimidating than the others Nemir had seen, but the way they were both looking at him now made him swallow nervously.

Memet glanced at Tuboy who was blatantly staring.

"He's kind of cute, isn't he?"

Instead of answering, Tuboy crawled over to Nemir, making him shrink away.

"You want more?" he asked gently.

Nemir gaped.

He hadn't thought that the ogres were capable of gentleness.

Not waiting for an answer, Tuboy pulled the wooden bowl from Nemir's stiff fingers and patted him softly on the head before crawling to the exit of the tent.

Memet grabbed his hand before he stepped out.

"Don't let any of the others see you being so sweet," he warned.

Tuboy just smiled at him.

As the tent flapped shut Memet sighed loudly and sprawled onto the ground with his eyes shut.

After a moment, he glanced at Nemir.

"You're safe for now," he said. "But don't think of running, or we'll really kill you."

"What do you want me for?" Nemir asked.

Memet smiled a little, his eyes drifting shut.

"If our demands aren't met, then Tasnia will have to deal with a war from our people, and now," he glanced at Nemir, "From yours as well, I guess."

Nemir's heart thumped in his chest.

"And if their army attacks you?" he asked.

Memet's smile widened.

"Let them," he said. "We'll kill them all in a thousand ways that they haven't ever prepared for."

Nemir shivered. Hearing the ogre's answers really weren't helping him, but he needed to know. Otherwise, being their captive was pointless.

"What are your demands for?" he asked uneasily.

"For the same rights as the elves, and the same aids as the humans," he said it easily, as though it was rehearsed and looked at Nemir, his smile widening. Did all of the ogres have such dangerous smiles? "We can live without both, but it's the principle."

Nemir stared in wonder. If it weren't for the recent warning echoing in his mind, and the fact that Memet had lain down straight across the entrance, he might have considered running. Memet and Tuboy didn't seem all *that* dangerous.

But then, the thought of all the other, more muscular, more frightening, much dirtier and much less gentle ogres came to mind and he took that thought back. For now, he would just do whatever they wanted him to do.

***

Desada stood on the port, her hair whipping wildly in the ocean wind. For the first time since she'd come to Tasnia, she could care less about her appearance.

She was furious, and the name of her fury was a particular blond haired prince, who wasn't even courteous enough to come see her off of his god forsaken country, when he'd gone and more or less *fed* her brother to a pack of hungry wolves.

"You're growling," Eliseo muttered softly.

"I don't care," Desada growled.

She marched up the plank and onto the ship, not waiting for anyone, not so much as waving goodbye to any of the dignitaries who had come to see her off.

If she was going back home, then she wasn't coming back until she had a fleet of war ships knocking at their door. First, she would destroy their stupid palace, and *especially* their stupid prince. Then, she would track down those ogres and rip them limb from limb. If her big brother had been harmed...

"Highness, you're room is this way—"

"Don't talk to me," she snapped.

She walked past the stunned lady in waiting and marched to the nearest empty room, under deck.

It was empty but for one rickety chair and a small desk. There were no windows, so she lit the oil lamp and sat rigidly with her arms crossed. Finally, after what felt like eternity, she felt the ship begin to move.

If they really waited for her and those damn Tasnian officials to get back to Suvahl, figure out what her family wanted to do and *then* return to Tasnia, then more than *two weeks* could have passed already.

Last year, Nemir had almost wet himself because an eagle had swooped down too close to him. Did they really think that he could survive two weeks?

Desada pushed herself up and marched rigidly back upstairs. She approached the railing, watching the Tasnian shore drift away.

They weren't moving too fast yet, but she'd have to act soon. First, she tied her hair back, then without a second thought, she yanked the fabric of her flouncy dress off of her shoulders, cursing when an arm got stuck. There was no time for buttons, so she tore along the seams.

"Everyone is staring, you know," a familiar voice said behind her.

"I—"

"Yes, I know," Eliseo interrupted. "You don't care."

"Exactly," she said.

She kicked the dress away from herself and looked at Eliseo.

"You tell my mother and father that I went to get Nemir back and if I were them, I would have a fleet of battle ships to the Tasnian shore the moment I could, because these good-for-nothing's need to discuss whether to *rescue* him or not on *twenty* different levels, before they do a damn thing!"

She hoisted herself up onto the railing.

"Good luck," Eliseo said with a smile.

"To you too," she said, throwing a glance at the Tasnian's, who had just realized what she was about to do.

She dropped back over the edge as the shouting started and hit the ice cold water, hard.

She took a moment to right herself and then she began to kick furiously toward the shore.

CHAPTER FIVE

S oluc couldn't wipe the grin off his face. This morning, he'd happily sent Shaw off to the palace, with the original message. It listed their demands and finished with a simple statement. *If you want the prince alive, you will meet our needs.* Somehow, with a new prince involved and the threat of another country, it sounded even more menacing than before.

"You're so lucky," he said, shaking his head. "I was *this* close to handing you off to Ilaj, and you know what he likes to do."

Lenroy just laughed.

"Things always work out for the best for us," he said.

"Not for me," Ilaj said, his eyes glinting. "Do you know how long it's been since I've had someone to play with?"

Lenroy laughed and smacked his arm.

"Just keep those teeth to yourself," he said. "Hey Tuboy!"

Soluc glanced over, finding his younger brother pulling little scraps of meat from the gazelle's bones.

Tuboy glanced over at them and made his way to where they sat, after collecting a few more pieces.

"You didn't congratulate me," Lenroy teased.

"Congratulations," Tuboy replied blankly.

"I bet you didn't trust your big brother to catch the human and bring it back still breathing, did you?"

Tuboy just shrugged.

"You hungry?" Soluc asked, changing the subject. He was sure he saw him eating last night, what was he doing getting more?

Tuboy shook his head.

"It's for the human," he said.

Ah yes, the little human who had made Soluc's entire being reek until he'd jumped in the river to rinse off the vomit.

"I'll take it to him," Soluc said, standing.

He took the bowl from his brother, squeezing his shoulder briefly, as he passed.

The twins were different from most of the oves, especially the ones under Soluc's command.

Their entire family was molded more by the elf blood in them, that was clear, but for the two of them, it was even more palpable.

He often wondered why Tuboy, in particular, chose to be a part of their militia, but he could only assume that it was to be near Memet.

Speaking of which, Soluc nearly tripped over Memet as he slid into the tent.

He stumbled and caught himself before glancing at the human, who was clutching the thin blanket to his chest in terror.

Soluc swallowed a laugh as best he could. He could only assume that the idea of being crushed by him was particularly horrifying.

"Oh, excellent," Memet muttered. "Destroy my new work *and* almost kill our bait."

Soluc knelt down with a grimace and glanced at Memet. Two of the new bones had slipped from their lovely neat pattern on his chest, and judging from the blood, some of the skin had ripped a little.

Memet sighed and pushed himself up.

"I'm going to go find Ilaj," he said.

"He's by the fire pit," Soluc called after him.

He turned back to the terrified human with a chuckle and offered him the bowl of food.

"I heard you're hungry," he said.

After a long moment, the prince reached out and snatched the bowl from his hand.

Soluc expected him to scarf it down, but the prince did not reach for handfuls, or press his face into the food.

He ate fast, but he dipped only a finger and thumb into the bowl, retrieving small pieces and placing them carefully into his small mouth. Soluc wouldn't have even known that he was hungry.

He had heard once that they ate constantly. Although, Soluc supposed that he didn't know all that much about humans.

"How often do humans eat?" he asked.

Prince Nemir looked up at him and swallowed.

"Three or four meals a day," he said.

"That much?" Soluc asked, surprised.

Prince Nemir nodded.

There was something about the little guy that made Soluc want to hear him speak more. He hadn't really registered the soft accent last night.

"How old are you?" he asked.

The human looked up at him guardedly.

"Why do you want to know all of this?" he asked.

He was clearly afraid, but his voice had a hint of brave, fierceness hidden behind it that Soluc found a little endearing.

Instead of smiling like he wanted to, Soluc narrowed his eyes.

"Just answer the question," he said.

The prince swallowed.

"I'm twenty one," he said at last.

Soluc nodded, finally letting the smile slip to his lips. Prince Nemir annunciated every sound so clearly.

Suddenly, he put the bowl down and looked up at Soluc with his large, unnaturally dark eyes.

"What are you going to do with me?" he asked softly.

His R's. Soluc had never heard any one do that rolly-thing before. Sort of like it just slipped off the tip of his tongue. Maybe it was the way they spoke in Suvahl.

He realized that the young man was waiting anxiously for an answer and cleared his throat.

"We sent a message to the palace already," he said. "We should receive a reply sometime today and then it's just a matter of setting you free."

Of course, he made it sound a lot easier than it was. There would still be negotiations to make, which might take days. Then they had to ensure that their needs would be met, and then after that, they had to safely return Prince Nemir to the palace in such a way that none of his men would be in danger.

Altogether, the prince would most likely be with them for a few weeks, but the little thing looked frightened enough as it was, without knowing the truth.

"I don't need to be bound until then, do I?" the prince asked uneasily.

Soluc glanced down at his small wrists, which he was rubbing carefully. There were thick bruises around both of them.

Surprised, he reached for his hands, pulling one out of the prince's grasp.

He stiffened in fear as Soluc examined the red and blue. Did all humans bruise so easily? He could have sworn that he hadn't tied the bindings so tightly.

"I promise I won't do anything as stupid as trying to run," Prince Nemir said.

Soluc looked at the fierce determination set on the prince's face and stifled another smile. He was brave for speaking so frankly, even when he was so scared.

He let go of his hands.

"You don't need to be bound," he said. He pushed himself up to his feet, as straight as he could in the tent. "Just be good."

"Wait!" Nemir shouted as Soluc took a step out of the tent.

He paused and looked back at the prince, whose face was an interesting shade of pink.

"I need to use the outhouse," he said.

This time, Soluc didn't bother trying to hide his amused smile.

"Sure thing," he said.

He stepped back, holding the tent open, while prince Nemir crawled toward him.

As he passed, he shot Soluc a look that said quite clearly that he didn't trust his amused expression.

"It's this way," Soluc said, leading him.

The prince followed uneasily as they tread through the camp. The oves that were around, all stared curiously until they passed into the trees.

"Don't rough him up too badly!" someone shouted and Soluc's grin only widened.

He shook his head and then finally stopped at a decent place.

He looked back at the prince, who had stopped a considerable distance away and was looking around wearily.

"Here we are," Soluc announced. "The outhouse!"

He laughed. *Outhouse*. It was a human expression that he'd heard once and had never been able to forget.

He snickered.

"We've been here for a week already, so it may be hard to find a clear spot. Just don't touch the ground."

Prince Nemir's eyes widened considerably, only making Soluc chuckle harder.

Finally, clenching his teeth, he walked to a large tree and turned to face it. He turned to look at Soluc over a shoulder.

"You can leave now," he said.

Soluc stared. There was no way the prince was that clueless.

"You're my prisoner," he said. "How am I supposed to leave you alone in the forest?"

Nemir's face turned that pink shade again but he frowned resolutely.

"Then turn around," he said.

Soluc raised a brow and did as he was told.
What did it matter if he saw the boy pissing?
He wondered.

There was a long silence and then finally, he heard the soft dribble of pee hitting tree — which stopped almost at once.

After another long pause, the prince sighed and Soluc heard him pulling his pants closed.

"You can turn around again," he said.

Soluc turned around and eyed the prince, who was looking very depressed.

"What's wrong?" he asked, as they began their walk back. Ever since Prince Nemir had arrived at their camp he'd been one of two emotions, determined or terrified. Depressed was new. And it didn't suit him.

Nemir sighed softly.

"I still need to go," he said.

Soluc raised a brow.

"You just went."

"I couldn't go with you listening," he insisted.

That was possibly the strangest thing that Soluc had ever heard.

He turned to look at the human but froze in his steps when he saw Lenroy, Shaw clinging happily to his shoulder.

Lenroy had a rolled scroll in his hand, the Tasnian official seal that had held it closed, already ripped apart.

The group surrounding his brother looked grim, but their eyes all shot to the human prince the moment he and Soluc drew near.

With a soft curse, Soluc marched up to his brother and snatched the letter from his hands. It was short. Too short.

He scanned it quickly and looked at the human, who had stopped farther away from the crowd of oves. He shrank down even smaller under their intent stares.

With a quick scan of those surrounding him, Soluc found Tuboy standing anxiously in the midst. He knew what was about to happen as much as Soluc did.

"Take him to the tent," Soluc said.

Tuboy hurried to follow his word.

"Stay with him," he whispered and watched as his brother snatched Nemir by the arm and pulled the confused prince away.

The rest of the oves had the surprising courtesy to wait before the questions began.

"I thought you said this was a done deal?" Lenroy finally asked.

Soluc took a breath.

"I didn't expect this," he said.

He pulled up the letter while the growling began and read aloud.

"'We need time to decide on a course of action...' What kind of humans would say that?" he demanded. "They're supposed to care about preserving their lives. That's a part of their species!"

His blood was pumping angrily through his veins.

"They'll be starting a war. I know that's not what they want."

"Clearly, you're wrong," Lenroy growled. "You don't know a thing about humans, do you?"

Soluc shot his brother a deathly glare.

"They try to protect each other," he growled back. "It's the strongest trait of their kind."

"Then they would have sent us a very obedient letter, meeting all of our demands and then some. They *want* a war!"

Everyone's clear consent made Soluc's hands shake. He didn't think the others realized just how much the humans could fight back.

"We should wait," he said.

"No!"

"They're planning something!"

"We'll be surrounded by hundreds of them within days," Lenroy said. "Why do you want to give them the upper hand?"

"I say we cut him to pieces and send him to the palace bit by bit while we prepare for battle!"

Cheering erupted at the suggestion. Soluc knew that cheer, he heard it every time blood was about to be spilled.

"No!" he shouted. He grabbed the one who'd shouted that by the cloth hung around her chest and hoisted her into the air. He threw her hard into the others, sending several of them tumbling to the ground.

Now that he had their attention…

"Nobody touches the human prince," he said. "I was left in charge of this mission and it's going to be done *my* way."

He looked around, trying to catch every single set of eyes and finally stopped at Lenroy.

"You don't know shit about humans," he said. "They don't want to kill their people, and if they put them against us, then they'll all be wiped out."

He pulled up the letter.

"This," he said, shaking it out for emphasis, "is just what it looks like. They're trying to be careful."

He took a deep breath, trying to calm his pounding heart. The rage coursing through his veins began to slow.

"We'll give them a time limit," he said at last. "And then, if they still don't meet it, we'll prepare for battle."

When no one responded, he simply turned and walked away.

Shaw followed him as he entered back into the trees, landing heavily onto his shoulder and rubbing her face against his long ear.

He walked and walked, wishing that the anger would abate entirely and he would be himself again. He looked at the letter one more time before ripping it to shreds and throwing it to the ground.

This was not the time to be swayed by his emotions. It was the ogre blood in all of them that drove them to illogical fury in a heartbeat, but the elf blood in him wanted desperately to think through their moves carefully.

The thought of sending pieces of Prince Nemir to the palace made his heart rate rush again and he sighed.

As long as they didn't hurt him until the time was right, then they still had a chance of securing a real home for the oves rather than their aimless wandering and cave dwelling. There was a difference between being nomadic by nature and simply settling, and the oves were doing the latter. They lived wherever they landed until it wasn't fit to house them anymore and then they moved. Always in the same areas, always avoiding their elf and ogre counterparts. Right now the oves were simply existing, not even allowed to have a permanent home according to the Tasnian law. They weren't citizens; they weren't even counted as animals.

If they did this right, then they could all live like Kings. Why was that so hard for everyone to understand?

CHAPTER SIX

Nemir was shaking from head to toe as the shouting continued. He was straining with all his might to make out what was being said, but could only catch a few words.

It was something about his imminent death, war and waiting.

Tuboy relaxed next to him, his long legs stretching out languidly, and began to pet Nemir's hair. Nemir didn't think he could take being here much longer.

"Lay down," Tuboy instructed softly.

Somehow, that seemed like an enormous trap, so Nemir stayed exactly as he was, anxiously sitting at full attention and fighting to make out the noises in the camp around him while Tuboy stroked his hair. It was extremely helpful being inside the tent. The flimsy white fabric made him feel safe.

The noise finally died down and Nemir sat in silence, hoping that he wouldn't pee himself. He wanted to tell Tuboy to stop touching him, but these ogres seemed to snap at a moment's notice and seemingly for no reason—and despite everything, the soft stroking motion was starting to relax him.

His head drooped and he found himself thinking wistfully of Desada.

If she had been captured, he doubted that these ogres would have made it all the way back to their camp with her and definitely not with all of their limbs attached.

He really should have taken more of an interest in combat sports, the way that she had.

***

Desada tied back her damp hair with a leather thong and considered her options.

She would need to track the beasts who had stolen her brother, starting from the field where they had been taken. It had rained not two days before her brother's fateful hunting trip and not at all since, so there was still a chance that prints were preserved in the soil.

Now the question was; since she had already stolen these worn pants, shirt and tattered short coat, along with an old bow and quiver, should she take it one step farther and steal one of the horses as well?

Desada looked up at the small house and then over at the deserted stable and shrugged.

She might as well, while she was here.

She had seen several people toiling in the wheat field she'd passed earlier, so she walked carelessly into the stable, knowing that no one would be there.

Only one horse was left unattended and free from duties in the field and Desada could instantly see why.

The old Mare looked battered and tired, probably a short ride from death.

With a grimace, she walked over to the poor thing, who glanced at her and snorted into her hair.

"Oh, you are a friendly girl, aren't you?" she asked. She stroked the mare's nose.

"Well, I don't have any treats for you," she said. "But do you think you could take me as far as the forest?"

She snorted again, and Desada took that as ascent.

Minutes later, she was riding at a painfully slow trot. She resigned herself to a slow ride, her thoughts drifting to Nemir.

One of the last things she'd said to her brother was, *they're ogres, do you honestly expect them to organize an attack?* And then she'd laughed in his face at his obvious fear.

She blinked the thought away. Now that her fury at the Tasnian's had mostly passed, she needed to focus on what was important; getting Nemir back.

She would have to be silent, quick, and stealthy. All talents, she was sure, the ogres would not expect, or even be able to comprehend.

The forest loomed into focus before her and Desada gaped at the density and size. She couldn't see where it started or ended.

The mare began to skip happily, her pace quickening as they trotted across the open fields.

"This will probably be easier on foot," Desada said, regretfully. She hopped off the mare and scratched her neck. "Enjoy your freedom, girl."

She took off as the mare began to graze and headed for the path she spotted that followed the curve of the forest.

With a heavy sigh, she scraped the heel of her leather boot across the path, marking her starting point, and began to walk.

She could only assume that the princes had been dragged into the forest and left some sign of scuffle, before Prince Allard had managed to escape.

For more than an hour she walked along the flat ground, her eyes glued to the earth, turning constantly left and right, for any sign. There were thin trails from wheels slipping off and on the path, hoof prints, and some prints from human shoes, but none that showed her anything abnormal.

Her stomach growled loudly and she shut her eyes. She didn't want to take the time to hunt. Not while her brother was out there.

With a sigh, she turned to the trees, marking a quick arrow onto the path to show her where to continue from. She could just find something small and edible, anything to hold her off until she was on his trail and able to afford some time for hunting food.

Desada took a step toward the trees and froze. That small tree, over there, was sitting at a very odd angle.

She edged toward it, finding it nearly snapped at the base. Some spots of the grass were also flattened oddly. Someone must have fallen there… and there.

Her heart skipping, Desada followed the trail straight into the trees.

A chunk of bark had been scraped off of a birch tree and then, after that, the clues became more subtle.

This must have been where Prince Allard had managed to escape.

She was impressed, despite herself, at how quickly he had gotten away. Most people would not have been able to do that. Then again, he was a royal knight and clearly, had his wits about him when it came to his profession. That much had always been clear in the way he stalked about in his chainmail and practiced endlessly with his sword.

Something snapped behind her and Desada froze. She listened to the light steps as they edged toward her, and with a practiced swiftness that she was famous for back home, she spun around, her sword in her hand and had the man pressed back against a tree, the sharp blade touching his neck, but not piercing it.

Bright blue eyes stared at Desada in disbelief.

"Princess Desada?" Prince Allard asked. "What are you doing here?"

She stared at him for a long moment, her eyes narrowing.

"You're the reason that I'm here," she said coldly. "If it wasn't for you, my brother would not have been carted off by bloodthirsty monsters."

She pressed the blade ever so slightly into his skin.

He gulped.

"I know," he said. "That's why I'm going to get him back."

***

Nemir tried as hard as he could to keep from waking up. It seemed that all he did lately was wake up to new and horrible things and he just didn't want to do it right now.

He snuggled under the thin cover and kept his eyes shut…

Why was it so quiet?

Grudgingly, he peeked an eye open, then abruptly sat up, scanning the tent in the dark. The fire light from somewhere distant in the camp was giving just enough light to see.

He was alone.

Why was he alone?

He hadn't been left alone for a single moment since he'd first woken up here, there was always one or more of the ogres sitting or standing uncomfortably close.

He crept to the door flap, his heart beat speeding painfully, and peeled it back.

The area was deserted.

The few tents that stood between him and the cover of the forest were still and quiet. Everyone was asleep.

He could escape.

The thought made his heart gallop at an uncomfortable speed. He would take the wilds of the night over the band of ogres any day.

It occurred to him that Tuboy had probably gone to the washroom and he had only moments to leave unnoticed. Taking a deep breath, Nemir climbed from the tent, keeping crouched low.

If anything approached him, he couldn't hear them over his pounding heart.

Just keep walking, he told himself.

The cold earth made little noise as he crept over it, step by step. The distance was farther than he remembered it to be. Why couldn't he just be there already?

Almost. He held back on whispering the word aloud. He was almost there.

Suddenly, two large shadows slid before him. Ogres.

Nemir stumbled back, a scream close to his lips and knocked into someone else. He spun around, realizing with a cold chill that he was surrounded.

A hand clamped over his mouth, stifling his scream.

"Where do you think you're going, squirt?"

It was him. The one who had caught him first. The one with the bright green eyes and frightening grin. Lenroy.

Even in the dark, he was terrifying. And the fact that Nemir didn't know what a 'squirt' was made it all the worse.

Nemir thrashed out wildly, receiving a light smack for all his efforts. He was hoisted up over a shoulder.

"This way," Lenroy said, leading the way.

Nemir inhaled a shuddering breath to scream but the ogre holding him chuckled softly.

"I wouldn't if I was you," she said. She didn't elaborate, but the tone of her voice brought more unpleasant images to Nemir's mind than he could count.

And why did he want to scream anyway? It would only draw *more* of them.

He was dropped to his feet, shaking, before the dim remnants of the fire.

"Good timing," Lenroy said, looking down at the embers and flickering flames.

Nemir looked around at the familiar faces. This was the very same group that had carried him all the way here, flung over one shoulder and clapped him hard on the head if he made a single noise or woke at all.

He swallowed hard, hoping that he wouldn't vomit again from fear. His stomach was already churning.

He took a breath. *Stay calm.* They couldn't hurt him. Soluc had told them not to. He had ordered it.

"Wh—what are you going to do?" he asked anyway.

His question only elicited quiet, snickering laughter.

Lenroy nodded to one of his followers and the yellow haired one who had been carrying him, came forward.

"You know what you're doing?" Lenroy asked her.

"I could do this in my sleep," she said and then suddenly, she was standing over him.

Nemir caught a flash of silver and yelped, jerking back wildly.

She backed off just as swiftly with a lock of Nemir's hair in her hand.

Lenroy held out another lock of hair, long and red, which meant it could be from several people's heads, including his own.

The yellow haired ogre took it and rubbed it together with Nemir's, whispering words that he could not hear, her eyes squeezed shut.

Then she held out a hand and dropped them into the dimming flames.

Nemir silently watched with the others as the strands caught fire and dissolved in the heat.

What was happening?

He looked back up at the female ogre just as she blew some sort of powder into his face.

Nemir promptly sneezed on her, which was rather gratifying.

She wiped her face with a grimace and handed Lenroy the small sack of powder that she had used.

"You know what to do," she said.

Lenroy nodded and took a menacing step toward Nemir.

"What's going on here?"

Nemir turned to the familiar voice, with a surprising rush of relief.

Tuboy and Memet both stood, as two threatening, mirror images, facing the others.

Tuboy reached out a hand for him. Nemir ran and grabbed it at once, feeling like a child when the large ogre pulled him behind him, protectively.

"Who took him out of our tent?" Memet demanded, narrowly.

Lenroy grinned, showing his teeth in that threatening way he did.

"We're just playing with him," he said. "It's not like we're torturing the thing."

Tuboy looked back at Nemir, carefully.

"Did they hurt you?" he asked softly.

Nemir bit his lip, thinking through the events. Aside from confusing him, they hadn't done a thing.

He shook his head.

The twins glanced over the group, nodding at their brother, before turning and leading Nemir away. How was it that the four brothers were all so different? Memet and Tuboy were oddly calming and comforting. Lenroy was downright terrifying. And Soluc was... Well, Nemir wasn't entirely sure about Soluc.

"What did they do?" Tuboy asked, once they were far enough away.

Nemir shook his head.

"I'm not sure," he said.

CHAPTER SEVEN

Soluc scratched his nose as he climbed out of his tent. It was another nice day, from what he could see. The early afternoon sky over their clearing was a pale blue, meaning unfortunately, yet again, there would be nothing to do for the day.

With a sigh, he stretched himself out, his bones cracking and popping back into place.

If he had known this job would require so much sitting around and waiting when the elders had offered it to him, then he doubted that he would have taken it. It was irritating.

And he was one of the patient ones.

He reached back into his tent, grabbing at the thin sheet of wolf skin he had flung aside the night before. He wrapped it familiarly around his hips and surveyed the camp.

It was getting more and more unkempt and haphazard, which said a lot. Tents were left, half collapsed and unattended, as everyone began to turn to one another for entertainment.

They couldn't stay here like this for much longer, or his oves would start looking for blood as their entertainment and it would most likely be the prince's.

Under most circumstances, Soluc wouldn't mind giving them what they wanted, but they needed the prince for now and they needed him alive. Then there was the fact that there was something incredibly fascinating about Prince Nemir that Soluc had yet to identify.

He wondered whether all humans had such an unguarded vulnerability to them. If so, it was surprising that they were so in control of the land and its creatures.

He walked into the cool shelter of the trees, stopping not too far off and pulling up his skins to pee. He wondered idly if the hunting party had left already, or if they would wait until later, as they had been doing lately.

"Soluc."

He glanced around at Memet with a brow raised.

His brother was too stealthy for his own good.

"One day you're going to end up with a knife in your throat for sneaking up on someone."

Memet smiled.

He pulled up the scant fabric that he had draped over himself and stood facing a nearby tree, relieving himself.

"Can I suggest that you tie up and gag the hunting team that captured Prince Nemir?" he asked.

Soluc straightened his wolf skin before addressing Memet with a raised brow.

"Why is that?" he asked.

"Because they're getting antsy with the prince's presence."

Soluc let the news churn in his head for a moment, processing it. It was nothing he didn't know already.

"Why the gags then?" he asked.

Memet smiled at him.

"For fun."

Soluc grinned and threw an arm about Memet's shoulders as they walked back.

"I am being serious though," Memet finally said. "Last night we found the little human, shaking in the center of the group of them."

Soluc stopped walking.

"Where were you when this happened?" he demanded.

"I was with some of the others and Tuboy just went to pee. When he came back, the prince was gone. He came to get me as soon as he saw that he was missing."

Soluc grimaced.

"Is he hurt?" he asked.

Memet, thankfully, shook his head.

"He's fine."

Soluc sighed and clapped him on the shoulder.

"Keep him safe for now," he said. "I'll come check on him later."

The camp was stirring now, everyone groggily rising to their feet and beginning their day. Soluc was glad at least, that they had burned though their liquor before they'd reached these grounds. If they were all drunk, as well as bored, the violence would have ended the little one last night, for sure.

He poked his head into Lenroy's tent, finding it empty and with a sigh, he sat and waited by the large fire pit for his other brother to emerge from wherever he spent the night.

Finally, long after the sun made its appearance above their grounds, Lenroy appeared.

He winked at Soluc, which only made him glower.

"Good morning brother," Lenroy said casually. "Why the long face?"

"You know perfectly well why," he said at once.

Lenroy exchanged an uneasy glance with Lamarr, the curvy blond who had followed him, with an arm around his waist.

"Do I?" he asked.

Soluc sighed.

He was sick of Lenroy's games, the way he spoke in circles.

"You carried off the little prince last night," he said simply. "Do you wanna tell me what you and your friends were doing with him?"

After a long, deep stare, Lenroy just shook his head, braking into a smile.

"Didn't the boys tell you?" he asked. "They interrupted our play time, and the little thing is right as rain."

Soluc nodded. It was true. Nothing had been done to Prince Nemir. He didn't even have a good excuse to smack that stupid grin off of Lenroy's face.

With a hard glare, he stood up and walked menacingly to his brother. He couldn't help it, menacing was what he did. He placed a hand tightly on his shoulder.

"Don't touch him again," he said.

Only after he passed, did Lenroy answer.

"I would be crazy to go against *you*, oh mighty one."

He heard Lamarr snicker and walked off with a sigh.

The hunters were only leaving now — which was frustrating. It was well past noon, which meant that unless they were really lucky, the whole camp wouldn't be eating—or would be eating late, at best.

He saw them off with an unfriendly wave, before turning and barking orders at the rest of the bystanders.

"Go refill all the water!" he shouted at a group that sat, conversing.

"Clean up the camp grounds!" he shouted at the rest.

He walked back to the fire pit, growling as he saw the number of oves sitting and laughing together.

"Go get firewood for tonight!"

They looked up at him, midway through a groan, saw his face and thought better of it.

It was mildly satisfying, watching everyone run to complete his tasks, but it wasn't enough.

Soluc walked through the arrangements of tents, poking his head into each one, looking for sleeping forms and snuggling couples and waking them mercilessly.

"Get up and fix all the tents," he ordered to each one.

He found Ilaj, sandwiched between two of the oves from yesterday's hunt, with angry looking scratches all down their sides.

Ilaj lifted a head sleepily and looked at him.

"Wreaking havoc so early in the morning?" he asked.

Soluc grimaced.

"It's past noon," he said. "And yes."

He looked at the other two and cleared his throat softly.

"Wake up!" he shouted.

Both of them jumped, making Ilaj laugh, as they fixed weary eyes on Soluc.

"Get up and help fix all the tents," he said.

"What?"

"Now!"

They both scurried up, hastily pulling on their boots and skins, while Ilaj ran his eyes over them appreciatively. Only after they left, did he turn his gaze to Soluc again.

"And what will you have *me* do?" he purred.

"Just supervise," Soluc said.

"And?"

Soluc sighed.

"And if they're misbehaving, then do whatever you'd like."

Ilaj smiled, exposing his sharpened teeth.

"You're a good friend to have," he said, as he hurried passed him.

He managed to laugh, as his friend went happily to his duty. Soluc went on looking for slackers but he paused as he came to Tuboy's tent.

He didn't know what this anxiousness, he was feeling, was. He had been told from several sources that Prince Nemir was safe and yet, he was afraid to even check.

Soluc was nervous to see him.

Pushing those thoughts away, he threw open the tent flap. He expected everything to be fine, but even so, his heart flipped in relief when he found Tuboy and Nemir sitting up in the tent, talking as though nothing at all was wrong.

Nemir looked up at him with his round dark eyes and Soluc's heart twisted.

"Is everything okay?" Soluc asked. His voice sounded possibly softer than he had ever heard it. He cleared his throat, chalking it up to all of the yelling.

Tuboy raised a brow silently and stood up.

"While you're here, I'm going to go get him some more food," he said, patting Soluc gently on the shoulder, as he passed.

Feeling suddenly awkward, Soluc eased himself down to sit a safe distance from the human.

"Have you heard back from the palace yet?" Nemir asked softly.

Soluc's mouth went dry.

He fought, for a moment, to speak and then cleared his throat again.

The human's voice had more of a melody to it than he had registered before.

"We've been corresponding," he finally said. Really, Soluc had sent Shaw back with a threat. He was giving the royals five full days to respond with their decision. Soluc was sure that it wouldn't be turned down, but for some reason, he didn't want to worry the prince.

"Oh."

Prince Nemir sighed softly and the soft touch of breath that reached Soluc's knee made his hairs rise.

He swallowed and looked down at the little thing.

Granted, Soluc had thought he was cute from the beginning, but this was different.

Nemir shifted uncomfortably and so did Soluc, adjusting his fur.

He looked away from the furrowed brows and soft blush touching the prince's cheeks but the sound of him shifting and wiggling did *not* make the matter any better.

What was wrong with him? This was a human. A *small* human. Soluc would probably rip the little thing in half if he ever *tried* to enter him and then his warning orders to leave the boy intact would be pretty useless.

Although, maybe it wouldn't be that bad. He'd known people who could accomplish amazing things with their bodies with enough practice...

"Soluc."

A hand clasped Soluc's wrist daringly, pulling him from his thoughts, the needy use of his name accompanied the action. Soluc's whole body stirred.

He leaned toward Nemir.

"Can you take me to the woods?" Nemir asked.

He wanted Soluc to let him free? He couldn't. Especially, not *just* because the human's hand was remarkably soft and warm.

Soluc wondered what it would feel like on other parts of his body and bit back a moan.

"I can't," he bit out.

Nemir looked like he was about to cry. His eyes glassed over.

"Why?" he demanded desperately. His fingers squeezed Soluc's flesh harder. "You can take me," he said. All of the blood in Soluc's body was officially abandoning its other posts. "I won't put up a fight this time."

This time? Had one of the others gotten to him? Tuboy perhaps? The thrill of anger that surged into Soluc didn't really make sense, especially concerning Tuboy. He wasn't the type to take advantage of someone. At least not someone so delicate.

What was wrong with him? Just days ago, Soluc hadn't been too bothered by the fact that the others were considering *killing* Prince Nemir, so why now—

"Please," Prince Nemir whispered desperately and Soluc's brain stopped working.

He reached out a hand and gently wove it into the prince's soft hair. It was even softer than Soluc remembered it being.

He leaned forward and the boy's eyes widened dramatically.

"Okay," Soluc whispered. "You don't need to beg, I'll do whatever you want me to do."

Nemir gasped as their lips touched.

His lips were soft, so soft, and warm.

But something was wrong. Why wasn't he kissing Soluc back? Why was his whole body frozen under Soluc's touch?

The warmth hit Soluc first and a moment later, the smell. He pulled back slowly and looked down, past Nemir's shocked and horrified face, to the wet spot in between his legs.

Soluc stared for a long moment as his brain cleared.

The human didn't want to have sex with him. He wanted to pee.

Of course. Why would he want Soluc? He would only rip him in half.

A breeze struck his back and he glanced at the tent flap as Tuboy entered with a bowl of meat and berries.

Tuboy paused at the entrance, his eyes running over the scene.

Soluc pushed himself up, not sparing the human another glance and pushed past his brother.

"Take him to the river to clean up," he snarled.

His whole body was jittering from what he had just done. Prince Nemir had looked horrified.

Soluc had never had an experience like that before. Normally, all kinds were happy to be Soluc's bed partner. He had never had to force a soul, like some did. Nor did he ever want to. He may be quick to anger, but he was just as quick to guilt.

Unfortunately.

Life would be so much easier if he just didn't care about the consequences of his actions or the effects they might have on others.

He caught sight of one of the younger oves, kicking logs into a pile.

"Hey!" he shouted.

The boy jumped hard and looked up at Soluc.

"Do it properly or you can get out of this camp!"

He glared at Soluc but went to the task, grudgingly doing as he was told.

Watching him closely, Soluc took a seat at the fire pit on one of the large, overturned logs with his arms crossed.

Everyone was doing as he'd instructed and he watched them with an iron glare to ensure that they would continue to do so.

After some time, Ilaj slinked up next to him and took a seat close to his side.

"You're in my bubble," Soluc said without looking at his raven haired friend.

Ilaj chuckled and rested an arm on his shoulder, making it worse.

"What has you in such a foul mood?" he asked.

Soluc turned a hot glare to him. Ilaj always pushed him far more than anyone else ever would. He knew that Soluc would never punish him for it. What was the point, when Ilaj would just enjoy it?

"Aren't you supposed to be supervising?" he asked.

Ilaj shrugged.

"I wanted to give you a visit," he said with a seductive smile.

In other words, he was hoping to get some entertainment from Soluc's anger.

Well, Soluc wouldn't give him what he wanted today.

He pushed up from his spot and marched off to Tuboy's tent again. He couldn't help it.

It was empty, the stale scent of urine permeated the whole place.

"Hey you!" he shouted to an oaf nearby, working on the tents. "Clean out this tent."

She stared at him coldly.

"I'm already fixing everyone's tents up. I'm not going to start cleaning them, too."

He narrowed his eyes.

"You will if you know what's good for you."

They watched each other coldly, neither stirring, until Soluc was sure for a moment that she wouldn't do as he said. He was a second from marching up to her and forcing her, face first, into the unfortunate mess that Nemir had left behind, but her shoulders sagged and she came forward to do his work.

He watched her do it, her shoulders tensed in anger the whole while.

He half expected the oaf to do or say something that would give him the excuse to smack her around unforgivably. But aside from a few annoyed huffs, she didn't say anything until she was done and walking away.

"Sleeping on a little piss wouldn't kill him," she muttered under her breath.

Soluc watched her go, blankly. He supposed it wasn't fair to take out his frustrations on innocent bystanders, despite how much he wanted to. Especially, when his frustrations were of a more carnal nature.

What he really needed, was someone to grace his bed tonight, or better yet, right now. He was sure he could find someone willing, but all he could think about was the little human, with the trembling voice and soft but surprisingly strong grip.

He glanced at the afternoon sky, noting how late it was getting, already.

Nemir and Tuboy should have been back from the river by now.

He glanced in the direction that they had gone and after a moment of deep deliberation, Soluc went after them.

CHAPTER EIGHT

N emir just looked at Tuboy. Initially, he'd thought that the ogre was gentle, considerate, an outcast and maybe even *kind*. But now he knew that none of those things were true.

First, he'd sneaked a peek at Nemir while he had been bathing, and now *this*.

"I am *not* wearing that," Nemir repeated sternly.

Sternness was probably wasted on someone so much larger and stronger than he was, but he absolutely refused.

Just looking at the thin strips of leather and fur made Nemir's cheeks heat. He had barely gotten use to gluing his eyes above shoulder level while dealing with his captors. There was no way that he could dress like them.

Tuboy stared at him for a moment, his brows furrowed in confusion.

"We don't often go around naked," he said. "But I suppose no one will really mind—"

Nemir's eyes widened.

"What?" he squeaked.

"You said you didn't want to wear these," Tuboy replied, indicating the small bundle of, what he called, clothing.

Nemir lowered in the water until his chin touched the softly flowing surface.

"That's not what I meant," he said. "I'm going to wear *my* clothes."

"But your clothes are dirty."

With a grimace, Nemir edged himself closer to the river bank.

"Turn around," he ordered, as the water began to thin.

Shooting Nemir another look, that informed him of his lack of sanity, Tuboy did as he was told.

Nemir shot out of the water for only an instant, grabbing the clothing that he'd hastily shed at the water's edge and with the bundle in his hands, he sank back into the icy depths.

Tuboy turned back around to watch as he began to scrub the mass of clothing.

One humiliation of this scale, was quite enough for one day, as far as Nemir was concerned.

Finally, deeming his trousers to be clean, he inched toward Tuboy and tossed him the bundle.

It sprayed Tuboy right across the face, before smacking wetly into his chest.

"Hang those up on that branch to dry," he ordered, ignoring the unimpressed eyebrow raise that Tuboy graced him with.

"Now you're acting like a real prince," he said, while he did as he was told.

From this angle, it was rather amusing how tall the ogres were.

Tuboy just looked ridiculously over grown. He barely had to reach his arms up to hang Nemir's clothes on the branches that Nemir would need to jump to reach.

He giggled and dipped his head, trying to muffle it in the cold water. Try explaining that to him. *You're so big that it looks silly.* Yes, that would go over well.

Tuboy suddenly stopped what he was doing and glanced in the direction of the camp.

He turned back to Nemir.

"You might want to take my advice seriously and put on these clothes while you still have the chance."

Nemir stared at him.

While he still had the chance?

"What do you mean by that?" he asked. He tried to sound haughty and unconcerned but his voice was shaking. He blamed it on the cold water but Tuboy didn't seem to notice.

He looked back toward the camp again and this time Nemir followed his gaze.

He heard the approaching footsteps only as Soluc became visible, marching angrily toward them.

Nemir sank deeper into the water, only exposed from the nose up, as the large hunkering beast drew to a stop before them.

Soluc did not look ridiculous *or* silly, Nemir amended. He was downright frightening.

He took one long look at Nemir and his eyes narrowed.

"You're still in the water?" he demanded. He turned to Tuboy. "What's taking so long?"

Tuboy smiled calmly.

"We're just waiting for his clothes to dry."

Soluc suddenly noticed the clothes hanging above him. His jaw dropped open and he shut his eyes, as though in pain, as the information processed.

Nemir shot Tuboy an angry look and the ogre just shrugged at him helplessly.

Soluc sighed heavily and pressed two fingers to his temple.

"Didn't you bring him anything else to wear?" he asked.

Tuboy nodded.

"Well yes but," he glanced at Nemir who was shaking his head furiously and then back at Soluc. "He won't wear them."

Soluc opened his eyes at that, seeing the furs, and fixed his gaze on Nemir.

At the intense stare, Nemir sank even farther under the water, so that only his eyes were visible.

Soluc just sighed again.

"Come out here and put this on," he said, tired.

Nemir shook his head. There was no way he was going anywhere *near* that creature.

Soluc raised a brow and took a step toward the water.

"I said come out here and put this on."

He kicked the bundle gently, unraveling the fur.

Nemir tried to calm himself, but couldn't. He remembered the way that—*creature* had pressed his full lips into Nemir's, as though he thought Nemir would *want* it.

Nemir shivered.

He couldn't let that ogre think it was okay, or he might try it again. He had to tell him off, which was just as well, because Nemir badly needed to come up for air.

He popped out of the water with a little splash and attempted to gasp up oxygen with some degree of dignity.

"Listen you," he finally said, "I'm not wearing what your people call clothes. There's not even enough of it for undergarments."

Soluc raised a dark brow, his expression dangerous.

"I think you've gotten too comfortable *Prince*. Do I need to remind you that you're our prisoner?"

Shaking, Nemir shook his head.

"I'm not wearing that stuff," he insisted.

Soluc's eyes narrowed dangerously.

"Get out of the water now, or I'm coming in to get you."

Nemir frowned.

He was bluffing. He must be.

"No," he said flatly.

There was a moment of stillness and then suddenly, Soluc was wading into the shallow depths.

"What are you doing?" Nemir demanded.

"What do you think?"

He jumped for Nemir, sending water spraying in all directions. Nemir dove out of the way.

"Stop!" he squealed, as he was carried away by one of Soluc's enormous waves. "I'll put them on!"

"Too late," Soluc growled.

A large hand closed around Nemir's ankle. He kicked out, screaming as he was pulled under.

Oh lord. He was going to die, wasn't he? Suddenly, he emerged, coughing and spluttering and landed on his belly over a hard shoulder.

Wheezing and struggling with all of the energy that he had left, Nemir was easily carted to the shore.

"Hand me the clothes," Soluc growled, as Nemir scratched him deeply down the expanse of his back.

"Put me down!" Nemir shouted.

Was Tuboy really just going to hand him away like this?

Tuboy had a clear view of Nemir's butt right now, didn't he?

The truth of his nakedness slowly dawned on Nemir and every drop of blood in his body, rushed toward his face.

He screamed.

"Stop that," Soluc growled. Then he smacked him. On his rear. His *naked* rear.

Nemir screamed, again.

Wait, what was he supposed shout, at times like these, when in need of a rescue?

"Fire!" he shouted at the top of his lungs.

"Stop that."

Soluc shook him.

Nemir took in a deep, ragged breath.

"Fire!" he bellowed.

"Stop shouting fire!"

"Fire!"

"Stop it!"

Nemir realized his mistake as they entered the camp. Whoever so daringly came to watch the fire, was greeted by the sight of Nemir's naked bottom.

He finally fell silent, as the snickering started.

"Hey Soluc, you left a hand print!"

"A hand print?" Nemir demanded.

The nerve.

If Nemir ever saw Prince Allard again, he would have to personally apologize to him. That little kiss to his hand barely seemed worth the slap that Nemir had given him for it.

Soluc ducked down into his tent, passed all of the curious bystanders who were grinning impishly.

Nemir squeezed his eyes shut, choosing to block them out. And then kept them shut, even when he was plopped down onto the semi-soft surface of Soluc's bedding.

He adjusted his legs, hoping it would shield his important bits from the ogre. A moment later, something soft dropped on top of his hips, to do the job more thoroughly.

Nemir peeked his eyes open, finding Soluc on his knees next to him, averting his eyes politely.

Nemir resisted the urge to snort at that.

"Put that on," Soluc said. "I won't watch."

Surprised, Nemir eyed the brute for a moment, trying to determine whether he was being honest. Although at this point, he supposed, it made no difference. He eased himself up, pulling the strip of leather with him.

He held it up, examining it. It looked like it had come from a deer or something like one judging by the fur, but he seriously doubted that it was enough to wrap around, or hide anything.

His cheeks heating yet again, he looked at Soluc, letting his eyes travel down the ogre's body.

He was fit, to say the least. Each muscle was well defined and toned under his tanned skin. It was all one perfect, sun shaded tone of brown, marred only by the piercings which adorned his body. Down each shoulder he had a thin line of rings, each of his nipples were pierced straight through with sharp, fang-like slivers of bone and four studs sat in his belly button. He had less than many of the others in the camp, but still enough to show his disregard for pain.

Nemir's mouth felt dry. He glanced down at his own naked body, swallowing.

What was wrong with him? He was supposed to be dressing himself, not ogling his captor.

Wait, he wasn't ogling. He refused to have been ogling.

"Are you going to put it on?" Soluc asked.

Nemir started.

"Yes, don't look," he said hurriedly.

With a quick glance at Soluc's 'clothing' which was what he was supposed to have been doing from the start, Nemir wrapped it around himself, tying it haphazardly.

He frowned down at the sight. He couldn't tell from this angle, but he was pretty certain that things were hanging out at the bottom.

"This isn't right," he muttered.

He pulled the front flap down, but it didn't seem to be making a difference. Maybe like this…?

The whole thing fell off.

Soluc chuckled.

"It's not funny…." Nemir trailed off, his eyes fixing on Soluc's face—which was facing him.

He squealed, pulling the fabric up to shield himself.

"Turn around," he said coldly.

Soluc was still smiling, an amused glint in his eyes.

"Just let me do it," he said. "It'll be over faster. Besides, I just had your junk pressed against my shoulder, so I don't see what it matters anymore."

Did he just call Nemir's genitalia *junk*?

"Come here," Soluc said.

When Nemir didn't move, Soluc crawled over and pulled the soft skins from his clenched hands. He didn't even look, as far as Nemir could tell, until he reached around him in a pseudo-embrace, wrapping the string part around him.

Nemir choked on his breath as Soluc suddenly cupped his genitals, adjusting him inside the soft leather. He slid a hand smoothly in between his thighs, the other snaking around, brushing over his backside before taking the string. He pulled his hand back through Nemir's legs, rubbing absolutely *everything* on his way.

Nemir tried to breathe, but there was simply no point when he was being stared at like that. No one had ever looked at him with such intent eyes.

Soluc suddenly wrapped both arms around Nemir's back.

For a moment he thought that he was being embraced, then realized belatedly that Soluc was just tying the last of the strings behind his back.

The device finally secured, he palmed Nemir's cheeks with hot hands and squeezed gently.

Under normal circumstances, Nemir was sure that he would be putting up a fight and telling the ogre to get his hands off of him. At the moment however, Nemir's ability to form words was taking a vacation and all he could do was squirm and make a strange high pitched sound in his throat.

Soluc did it again and this time Nemir took a shuddering breath.

This was definitely not right. Nemir was mortified by his reaction to having his backside massaged by the strong hands. But at the moment, all blood that would normally go toward showing his embarrassment with flushed cheeks, was shooting through his body to fulfill another task.

He should stop this while he still could.

Nemir reached up, intending to push the ogre away, but just then, Soluc removed a hand from Nemir's bare backside and swiftly pressed it against the front of his new skins.

Nemir moaned, his head dipping back slightly, and instead of pushing Soluc away, his hands pushed into Soluc's chest and gripped him.

The sharp tips of his nipple jewelry cut into Nemir's palms.

He gasped.

Taking the invitation, Soluc dropped his lips to Nemir's open mouth.

Somehow, Nemir didn't mind it nearly as much as he had this afternoon, probably due in large part to the fact that his bladder was not about to explode.

Soluc's tongue delved into his mouth, tasting him and Nemir moaned again.

The carefully tied thong dug into his flesh for a moment and then fell away, leaving cold air rushing at Nemir's still damp flesh.

He looked down in a daze, realizing that Soluc had ripped it off of him and was accosted by the sight of himself brazenly aroused and straining to be touched.

Soluc tugged him into his chest and the object of Nemir's thoughts slid in between Soluc's legs.

The ogre squeezed his thighs together around him. Nemir arched into the heat, despite himself, and was rewarded by a mouth dropping over his own, sucking on him mercilessly.

With trembling hands, Soluc pulled away and pushed Nemir flat onto his back.

He lay there, dazed for a moment, his erection standing at attention in between them as he watched Soluc yank his own clothes from his body.

What was happening?

Before thoughts could overtake him, Soluc crawled over him, his long hair running tantalizingly up Nemir's body until their faces were even.

Soluc bent down, placing a soft kiss against Nemir's lips as he settled on top of him.

His weight felt good, not too heavy, but more than enough for Nemir's erection to be jammed against the larger man's belly, offering him some relief.

Something hard scraped against his tip, making him gasp. It took Nemir a long moment to realize that it was the belly button piercings that he had spent so much time admiring.

He tilted his hips, trying to reproduce the sensation and moaned again, when he did.

Soluc chuckled into his neck, sucking a little spot there before sliding lower, trailing kisses down Nemir's body. He paused at a nipple to suck it softly before he was moving down farther.

His tongue didn't stop until he was at Nemir's 'junk'. Soluc lifted his head, his eyes hungrily taking in the sight before he bent over it.

His long, auburn hair, hung down like a curtain, blocking his lips from view as they closed around Nemir.

He gasped, his whole body arching into the soft wet heat above him.

His hands reached out, spastically gripping into Soluc's hair. His whole body was shaking—and then Soluc stopped.

He pulled away and before Nemir could summon the words to argue, he dipped his head back down again, tracing his tongue farther down.

Nemir's eyes widened. He tried to sit up but Soluc pushed him back down.

"What are you doing—ah!"

All arguments vanished from Nemir's being and he arched, shoving and pressing for Soluc's tongue to enter him farther.

Soluc chuckled against him breathily, then returned to his task, moaning hungrily as he continued his work.

As Nemir's body began to tense, his breaths coming in raspy, uneven gasps, Soluc pulled away.

Disappointed again, Nemir wondered vaguely if this was some kind of ogre torture.

Soluc straightened, lifting above Nemir, stroking himself with eager hands, his eyes eating up the sight of Nemir, laying under him, as he did.

Finally, he inched forward.

Nemir only realized what Soluc was about to do when he positioned himself at his entrance.

His eyes widened.

This was not going to work, not when Soluc was so large.

Before he could argue, Soluc pushed forward gently, but insistently, and just like that, Nemir's body opened around him.

He cried out at the large, burning intrusion.

"Shh," Soluc whispered. "Just relax."

Easy for him to say.

He gripped Nemir by the knees, pushing his legs up and that helped, but it wasn't enough.

"It hurts," he cried.

"It's okay," Soluc gasped. "Just a little more."

He pushed, leaning over him until they were fully pressed together.

"It hurts," he said again.

The look of regret on Soluc's face was enough for Nemir to wish that he loved it, but he didn't. It felt hard and intrusive and painful.

Then Soluc moved.

He gasped at the friction, confused as to whether that was pleasure or pain.

"I'll make you like it," Soluc gasped.

He angled himself, adjusting Nemir's legs and wiggled ever so slightly and carefully.

Nemir gasped.

Okay, that was different.

Soluc continued to wiggle into him with soft short little thrusts until they didn't feel so foreign anymore.

Then he hit something that made Nemir's head drop back with a cry.

"There we go," Soluc whispered roughly. He pulled out slowly and jammed back in, making spots explode before Nemir's eyes.

He thrust into him, the speed picking up, the sound of their skin slapping together filling the tent until Nemir's entire body clenched.

He strained against Soluc as he spilled all over himself.

"Just a bit more, okay?" Soluc asked.

Nemir couldn't think of any reason at all to argue with him. The ogre felt like he was made to be there.

He took up the rhythm again, thrusting into Nemir's small, tight body. With one final hard pounding, his body stiffened over him and Nemir felt warmth spill into him.

Soluc's body relaxed and after a few languid thrusts, he pulled out of him, collapsing next to him on the thin bedding.

It was funny. Now that they were done, it was almost like a piece of him was missing.

The ogre wrapped an arm around the human and pulled him into his embrace, tightly.

"I've wanted to do that all day," Soluc whispered and Nemir finally realized, he did too.

CHAPTER NINE

Desada sat down listlessly on a low hanging branch. The whole tree swayed under her weight, but she barely noticed.

"Would you like to camp?" Allard asked. It was clear that the woman was finally feeling the effects of traveling the way they were, but he didn't mention it. He was a gentleman, after all.

She looked up at him with her large, dark eyes. They were remarkably like her brother's, the same spark in both of them, which oddly enough, read as curiosity in Desada where it read as uncertainty in Nemir.

They had been travelling non-stop since they'd set out after Nemir. They were almost there; Allard could feel it in his very bones.

He was frighteningly intuitive; hence his talent in hunting but Desada didn't seem very interested in his talents, choosing only to shoot him angry glares whenever their eyes met.

She didn't bother with that now, though.

"It's been too long," she said simply.

Truth be told, he preferred her anger, to the look she was giving him now.

Allard propped himself down before her, forcing her to look into his deep blue eyes.

"No," he said. "They're keeping Nemir alive, they said so in their ransom."

"How do you know?" she asked. "Maybe they were tired of waiting for a reasonable response from your people. Maybe they *want* to cause a war."

He reached out a hand and placed it gently on hers.

"Let's keep going," he said. "We'll find them by night fall—morning at latest—and I vow on my manhood to get your brother back alive."

Desada's eyes widened a little, her lips tilting for some reason into an amused smile and she nodded.

He often said things that sounded the way a prince's words should; confident, poetic, foreboding, but they weren't always true. Allard thought of Prince Nemir, the way his hand had stung across his face shamelessly, when no one in his entire life had dared to harm him. He thought of his laugh and the way his eyes had lit up when they'd come to their truce. He had only known Desada's brother for three days, but this time, he knew he meant his words.

Unfortunately, her fears were a stark possibility. Allard tried not to think of the fact that, by now, Nemir could very well already be dead.

***

Nemir wished he was dead.

Soluc adjusted himself, squeezing Nemir and dragging his lips along his round, human ears before sighing into his hair, his breathing evening again.

Yes, Nemir definitely wished that he was dead right now.

He was pretty sure that it was morning, judging by the tweet of birds in the trees and he really didn't want to know how he had slept for so long. And he *definitely* didn't want to think about the fact that they had been lying like this for a whole night.

He shifted ever so slightly, wondering if he could ease himself from the ogre's embrace without waking him, but shut his eyes when his bottom stung from the effort.

He groaned, squeezing his eyes shut, his whole face catching on fire.

He felt sick. Not just upset with himself, but genuinely like he was going to hurl all over the large, man-like being, currently snuggling him.

This time, the sting of tears burning his eyes had nothing to do with fear for his life.

He was ashamed of himself.

Footsteps crunched in the twigs and soil just outside the tent and Nemir shrank down under Soluc's large arm. They grew faint and he sighed in relief.

His heart was pounding from the threat of an encounter. He was dreading one of the others coming into the tent without warning, as they all seemed to do. Even more than that though, he was dreading the eventuality of Soluc waking up.

What if he wanted to do—what they had done—again? What if Soluc acted like they were lovers, or worse, went back to treating Nemir like a piece of property to be bossed around?

As gently as he could, Nemir turned toward the ogre, only managing, by planting himself against the muscular chest.

One of the little piercings there dug into his shoulder and he remembered with sudden clarity the feel of it pressing sharply into his palm.

He squeezed his eyes shut again with a shudder, fiercely attempting to erase that memory from his mind. His thoughts soared over many different, boring subjects that he'd been forced to study over the years, but none of them seemed to be quite enough.

Finally, it started to work, his body's embarrassing reaction to the memory slowly softening.

Soluc sighed contentedly in his ear.

Nemir opened his eyes, his forced train of thought disappearing. For the first time, he realized that Soluc's long silky hair was draped over his waist, sliding against his skin a little, every time he inhaled and exhaled.

It hung like a curtain over Soluc's face and Nemir wondered how on earth the ogres could stand having it so long.

He reached out and gently brushed the strands away from Soluc's face, exposing the sharp line of his nose and jaw and the soft full curve of his lips.

His heart was pounding again. He watched the ogre's closed eye lids for a moment, wondering if he could feel the steady beating since they were pressed so close together, but Soluc didn't even stir.

Suddenly, feeling irrationally relaxed, Nemir rested his head back onto Soluc's arm and continued his silent appraisal of the half ogre.

It was a wonder that everyone referred to them as that. In fact, they looked more like large humans to Nemir. Everyone, including the women towered over a foot taller than him. They all seemed to be gifted with a naturally limber and muscular physique, and if he was being honest, they had nice faces too.

Although Soluc's was the nicest of all.

He blushed a little at the thought and then reprimanded himself for it. He was the only one who could hear himself think, so what did it matter if he was being honest with himself?

Soluc was handsome. He had large kind eyes, set in a fierce frame. He was frightening and quick to anger but he was also more rational than most of the others. He smiled at Nemir and was gentle with him and despite his hard, muscular body, when he held him, it felt soft.

Nemir's body was stirring again, remembering just how considerate Soluc could be.

He reached out gently, and as softly as he could, traced a thumb over Soluc's lips. They were so soft.

"Hey, Soluc!"

Nemir jumped, hard.

"Stop slacking and come out here!"

Frozen, Nemir stared at Soluc as his eyes opened groggily, and fixed on him, looking surprised.

After a moment, he blinked and looked toward the voice.

"Go away, Lenroy!"

The tent flap flew open without warning and Soluc's brother stuck his head in with a growl.

"Soluc," he said sternly. "You can fuck around later, something happened."

Soluc watched Lenroy for a long moment, ignoring the shocked human laying in his arms. Finally, he nodded.

Lenroy was gone instantly, but the damage had been done. Nemir desperately wished the ogres had just killed him when they'd first caught him. He'd rather that than being seen this.

And Lenroy hadn't looked surprised or anything… did they all know?

He realized the ease with which he could hear the camp's activities and thought that he might not need anyone to do the job for him. He was about to die from embarrassment all on his own. He had been practically screaming.

"What's wrong?" Soluc asked, sitting up.

Nemir became suddenly aware of how naked he was and any ability to form words promptly vanished.

Ignoring him anyway, Soluc quickly tied up his coverings. Nemir looked away until he was done and then kept his eyes averted, just in case. Soluc dropped down over him and pressed a chaste kiss against the corner of his lips.

"I'll be back soon," he said with a soft smile.

He ruffled Nemir's hair roughly and was gone.

Nemir laid in stunned silence for a moment, his stomach twisting as an after effect of the kiss that had barely touched his lips.

He lifted a hand to touch the spot, but stopped himself.

"What is wrong with me?"

"I think *I* have an answer for that."

Nemir started, violently. He shot into a sitting position when he saw who it was.

The blond who had been so glued to Lenroy's side the other night, leered into the tent at him. Nemir had heard the others call her Lamarr.

He tried in vain to cover his nudity with his hands and then gave up, clutching the rags of animal skin over his groin in an attempt to hide himself from her.

She smiled down at him and arched a brow in a particularly irritating way. Then she entered the tent fully and sank down, cross-legged, across from him.

"You got to know our *wise* leader very well, from what I heard," she said simply. "So tell me, what do you think of him?"

Nemir scowled. He didn't need to be in a crown to know when someone below his station was speaking down to him, and he didn't need to be in love to know that his—*actions*—were being insulted.

"What do you want?" he snapped.

"Feeling feisty, are you?" she asked with a twisted grin. "I was hoping you would be."

She moved so fast that Nemir barely had the chance to squeak before he was flung over her large shoulder.

"What are you doing?!" he demanded, as she carried him through the tent exit. "Soluc said not to touch me!"

"Did he now?" someone asked, popping up at his side. "And why does Soluc get to have all the fun?"

Nemir was smacked so hard on the rear that his eyes stung and then to his horror, the ogre soothed the spot, running a hand over it. He squeezed his cheek, hard.

"Stop it!" Nemir shouted.

He fought for control, but there was no point, Lamarr was too strong.

What were they going to do with him? Were they going to murder him? Or worse, were they going to rape him?

He couldn't breathe.

He barely heard the next shouted words over the sound of blood rushing through his ears.

"Who wants to see a little human being fed to the wolves?" Lamarr shouted.

What did she mean? Were they really going to feed him to *wolves*? Regardless of the specifics, Nemir wanted none of it.

"No!" he shouted.

The humiliation of being hung upside down naked, seemed to have worn off since yesterday, especially in light of the fact that he was likely about to die.

He could care less about clothes right now.

"Let me down!" he screamed. "I'll kill you!"

He ignored the laughter and swung out his arms, attempting to hit any of the bodies that were near.

Suddenly, Nemir was dropped to the ground.

He tumbled flat onto his back. His head swimming from the impact, Nemir stared up at the sky for a long moment.

It was blue today, not a cloud in sight. It was exactly the type of day that he loved to sit outside in the garden. What would his old self say, if he'd seen this moment? Nemir couldn't even imagine.

"What are you doing?"

A thrill of hope ran through Nemir and he lifted his head slowly, finding Tuboy squeezing himself into the circle of ogres.

He stepped up to Nemir, ignoring the others with a determined set to his face and reached out a hand to help him up.

Nemir reached for it, but two others stepped in between them, shoving Tuboy back.

"I don't think so," Lamarr said.

She turned in a slow circle, looking at the others in the camp.

"Who here wants to stir things up a bit?" she asked loudly. "Who wants to start a war?"

The oves cheered.

Nemir's entire body went cold as everyone turned to face him.

If that was what they wanted, then just one little human's death would grant them their wish.

CHAPTER TEN

"Lenroy, what the hell is going on?"
Soluc planted his feet into the soft,
forest earth and crossed his arms until
his brother grudgingly stopped.

He turned to face Soluc slowly, a stricken
look on his face.

"Something happened," he said.

Soluc growled, the sound rumbling deep in
his chest.

"So you've said," he retorted. "How many
times have you said that now? Four times? Five?"

Lenroy frowned.

"Let's just keep going. You'll see when we
get there."

He turned to continue on, but Soluc
gripped his shoulder, stopping him. He dug his

nails into his brother's flesh, making him hiss in pain.

"I don't think so. You tell me what's going on now, or I'm walking back to camp and cozying up next to the human and going back to sleep."

Lenroy's face paled.

"Don't," he said, seriously.

Soluc frowned.

"Why?" he asked.

"Someone's been hurt," Lenroy admitted. "I don't think they'll make it for much longer. I thought you should know before the rest."

Soluc's eyes narrowed. Lenroy wasn't the type to play practical jokes like this. Soluc had only ever seen Lenroy so serious on the day that their mother and father had died.

He simply nodded and followed Lenroy, who continued walking with a relieved sigh.

Soluc's mind raced through the possibilities. Who would Lenroy be so concerned about that he would come to tell Soluc ahead of everyone else?

The first person to rush to the forefront of his mind was Nemir—which was ridiculous on a variety of levels, the most important of which being that he had just been snuggled up to the human's warm side. He knew that Nemir was safe. Not to mention the fact that Lenroy would probably be ecstatic by the human's demise.

The thought made his heart twist unpleasantly. Soluc pushed the feeling aside.

Nemir was fine. Someone else was hurt.

It didn't make sense though. The few people that Soluc would consider his friends, Lenroy didn't care all that much for, and of them, only Ilaj, Memet, Tuboy and Lenroy had left the mountains with them.

Soluc quickened his step, thinking of them. He hadn't spared a glance around the camp as he'd left. He didn't know who was there, or if any of them had gone on the hunt.

"Did you leave with the hunt today?" he asked.

Lenroy glanced at him.

"No," he said. "Why?"

Something wasn't right. Why would Lenroy be alone to witness the accident that would leave one of his friends near death?

"It shouldn't be long now," Lenroy finally said.

The grim tone of his voice made the hairs rise all down Soluc's arms. They began to slow down and Soluc raked the area for a sign of scuffle, for anything, but there was nothing here.

Lenroy slowed to a stop. He took a deep breath and then turned to look at his brother.

"I'm sorry," he said.

"What's going on?" Soluc asked, slowly.

Lenroy shook his head.

"You'll know soon enough."

As though on cue, a sharp pain rang through Soluc's right arm.

He gasped and reached for it, sure for a blinding moment that something was crushing it.

Suddenly, the pain passed.

Soluc stared down at his arm. It looked normal. He wiggled his fingers and gripped it tightly in his other hand, but it was completely normal.

Slowly, he straightened himself.

He looked down at his little brother, breathing heavily from the momentary pain.

It was magic. Some form of twisted magic, Soluc was sure of it. And however the brat had figured out how to do it, he was going to pay.

"What did you do?" he demanded.

"You pushed us to this," Lenroy said, ignoring the question.

"Us?" Soluc asked.

"Me, and a few of the others," he answered simply. "You know as well as we do, Soluc. You're not fit to be the leader. You're sucking the life out of the whole team."

"Stop talking shit, Lenroy."

He stepped forward, his hand shooting out and snatching his brother's neck. He yanked him closer, so their faces were almost touching. He opened his mouth to speak but a sharp cry of pain came out instead.

He tumbled to the ground, clutching his thigh until the phantom pain began to pass.

What was this? What was happening?

"We're not elves, Soluc, and we sure as hell aren't humans." Lenroy's bright eyes sharpened as he spoke. "It's *your* fault for trying to make us act like them."

"Lenroy," Soluc gasped. "Stop this."

He pushed himself unsteadily to his feet. His leg felt weak, like it was healing from a bad wound.

"I can't," Lenroy said, "and neither can you."

Soluc stumbled forward into Lenroy's arms. His brother caught him as he felt like his head had been smashed in from the back.

Lenroy let him drop to the ground.

Was he really going to die? Was his brother really going to kill him?

He would never see Nemir again if that happened, and never, among other things, get to relive last night.

The stars before Soluc's eyes began to clear.

Why was he thinking about the human prince when his life was possibly about to end?

Soluc blinked the last of stars away but didn't get up. He stared up at the bright blue sky.

The afternoon sun was just lifting above them, becoming visible through the canopy of leaves, but despite the growing warmth of the day, a chill ran through Soluc's body.

Nemir—they had taken him and done something to him the other night but they hadn't hurt him and then—then the next day, Soluc had been so on edge and he had wanted the human— he'd wanted him so badly…

He pushed himself up and looked at his brother, stunned. The phantom pain suddenly wasn't so magical. It was a spell he knew well from being a part of oaf society his whole life.

Soluc was feeling the pain, but Nemir was the one truly experiencing it.

"You're killing us," he said. "Both at the same time."

Lenroy frowned.

"I was hoping you'd be dead before you figured it out." He sighed. "Oh well, it won't be long now."

Soluc jumped to his feet.

His first instinct was to rip his brother limb from limb—but Nemir…

He spun on his heel and took off into the trees, back in the direction that they'd come from.

"You'll both be dead before you get there!" Lenroy shouted after him.

No. It was true that they didn't take long to finish someone once they'd started, but Nemir would make it.

"Please," he whispered.

His thighs burned as he pushed himself on at breakneck speed. He cursed the amount of time it had been since he'd been hunting and pressed on harder.

He was almost there. He could hear the shouting over the sound of rushing wind through his ears.

He was almost there and he was still alive. Good sign.

Tasting the excitement in the air, Soluc broke into the camp ground. The shouting was from around the fire pits.

Soluc forced himself on toward it and stumbled with a little hiss when his toe surged with pain.

Soluc paused. Had someone stepped on Nemir's toe?

That wasn't right. It didn't sound like any form of torture that he was familiar with.

Cautiously now, Soluc continued on, but he stopped being so careful when he emerged from behind the last of the tents. He stared in awe at the mess.

Everyone was fighting. Not just the usual few, but literally *everyone*.

"Stop it!" Lamarr screeched, jumping to her feet in the center. "Stop it! We need to kill the human!"

Soluc couldn't help but smile.

Lenroy and his friends might think they knew their people, but they didn't know them, not nearly as well as Soluc did. It wasn't war in particular that they wanted. They were just itching for a fight, and Lenroy was offering it to them.

Lamarr's eyes met his and he grimaced.

Oops.

"You!" she shouted.

She jumped toward Soluc, brandishing her long, rusted sword. He swung out of the way at the last moment, her blade catching on the strands of his hair.

"Where's Nemir?" he demanded.

She spat, slicing into his arm.

As blood rushed from Soluc's body, a searing anger flowed through him.

With a cry, he jumped at the oaf. He shoved her blade aside and struck her across the jaw so hard that he heard a crack. She landed on the ground with a thump and didn't move.

Soluc's whole body was shaking. This wasn't good. His anger was overtaking him. He wanted to rip all these idiots into pieces; his fingers were itching to do it.

A loud scream pierced his thoughts.

Nemir.

A touch of sanity cleared Soluc's mind and he took off, shoving oves aside, and kicking them out of the way.

There. Several people stood surrounding something and Soluc could only assume that it was Nemir, about to have his life extinguished, along with Soluc's.

Soluc grabbed the first oaf that he could reach, sending him tumbling to the ground in moments.

Everyone turned surprised eyes up at him.

For a stunned moment, Soluc stared at Tuboy and Memet who stood towering over Nemir, but he quickly realized that they were protecting his human.

"Soluc," Nemir said in a shaking voice. The note made Soluc's heart twist.

With a roar, he turned on those around him, swinging in each direction he could, his fists meeting skin almost without fail.

He was struck on the back of the head hard and stumbled forward.

"Take him," Tuboy said, shoving the prince into his arms. Without waiting for a response, Tuboy jumped out, landing on top of the oaf behind Soluc and pummeling her face.

Nemir looked up at him with dark, terrified eyes. His leg was cut open and bleeding just where Soluc had felt the searing pain. Shaking, he stooped down and swung Nemir onto his shoulder.

Any weakness that his legs had felt before, vanished as he hoisted Nemir up.

One of the younger oaf's jumped at him and Soluc kicked him hard in the nuts just because he needed something to make him laugh right now.

And also because he deserved it.

Soluc spared one quick glance for the twins, his loyal brothers, who were kicking ass, if he did say so himself, and ran.

As he cleared the camp, he was tempted to deposit Nemir and go back, but Soluc just couldn't put his life in danger, or Nemir's would be too.

He kept on blindly, until the sounds of his people destroying one another faded into the distance and only the creaking and rustling of the forest could be heard.

"I can't breathe," Nemir muttered.

Soluc had almost forgotten about the boy's uncomfortable position, flung over his shoulder.

Carefully, he slid Nemir down, blood dragging across his chest as he did.

Nemir's feet touched the ground and he wobbled dangerously.

"Are you okay?" Soluc asked gently.

Nemir looked up at him hazily.

"Okay?" he asked quietly. "Am I okay?"

Soluc swallowed.

"I was kidnapped by a bunch of ogres! They tried to kill me and barely fed me and wouldn't let me pee and had sex with me!"

His voice echoed through the trees hysterically. Soluc grimaced. It did sound pretty bad when he said it that way, but there was one more thing.

Nemir took several shallow, panicked breaths.

"Am I okay?!" he demanded again. He shoved Soluc's shoulder hard. I'm stranded in the middle of the forest and I'm bleeding and I'm *naked*!"

Soluc ran his eyes over Nemir's slender form and nodded. The human did seem to have a problem with nudity, but judging by his rant, he didn't know the most important part of all this, yet.

"That's all true," Soluc said slowly. "But there's something else."

"What is that?" he demanded shrilly.

Hm. How to best word this?

"You're married, too."

Nemir blinked at him, startled.

"What?"

"When they took you to the fire that night? I'm guessing that they burned some of your hair, along with someone else's?"

Nemir nodded slowly.

"That's the Elvin marriage ritual. Our people do the same thing. It means that you're—well bound to someone I suppose. Although, I've never heard of it being done without a ceremony or both people there, at least."

Nemir's face was frighteningly pale.

"I'm married?" he asked slowly.

Soluc nodded.

"To who?"

Soluc smiled awkwardly.

"Well, me obviously."

Nemir stared at him for a good long moment and then bent over and puked.

Soluc jumped out of the way, barely saving his toes, and sighed. The human had some bad habits when he was upset.

Nemir took several gasping breaths and then looked up at Soluc, tears streaming from his eyes.

"Are you joking?" he asked.

Soluc swallowed. Was it really such bad news to be hitched to him?

He simply shook his head and stared as the boy erupted into tears. He watched for a moment, overtaken by a desperate desire to make Nemir happy.

"Do you want my loin cloth?" he asked.

Nemir looked up at him startled, and then down at the offered garment and began to cry even harder.

CHAPTER ELEVEN

Prince Allard whipped the sword from his belt, the metal catching a glint of light and reflecting off of the trees around them.

He took a step forward and Desada let an arrow whiz by his nose, striking the trunk just past him with a hallow thud.

His eyes wide, he spun to face Desada. Her bow was still swinging in her grip.

She held back a smile at his stunned expression.

"Do you want to die, Prince?" she asked coyly.

"P—pardon me?" he sputtered.

She smiled darkly.

"I didn't think so. Which is why you should put that damn sword away and don't step a foot into that oaf camp, whether you feel compelled to, or not."

Continuing to stare, he whipped off his uncomfortable looking helmet and dropped it to the ground.

"We came all this way," he said advancing on her. "I'm not leaving until we tear their tents apart and find your brother."

Desada grimaced, but didn't back down.

"You think they're in a state to be kind to us?" she asked.

Together, they turned back to the commotion of the camp. They were a safe distance away, hidden by the trees, but even from here they could easily hear the ruckus.

She sighed and glanced up at Allard. His blue eyes were darkened by their travel and the usual flow of his movements was disturbed by his heavy limbs.

"We should wait," she said. "At least until they've slept, and then we can sneak in and look for him."

Allard clenched his fists, but he didn't argue.

With an overly anguished sigh, he dropped back against a tree.

"Let's just wait here then," he said.

Desada nodded.

She eased herself down against another large tree, the rough bark scraping her back as she slid down. Her whole body was sore, but it was hard to sit still like this. She wanted nothing more than to follow Prince Allard's lead and run screaming into the horde of vicious beasts, weapons drawn, but there was just no point in that.

They weren't on a suicide mission.

She shut her eyes for only a moment, but when she opened them again, they fixed on a pair of knees.

A pair of very large, *naked* knees.

As though they were glued in position, she had to drag her eyes up the form. Up the long, tanned, shapely legs—which were entirely exposed—to the beige rag, wrapped around trim hips, up a washboard abdomen and smooth chest, all the way to a face.

Her breath caught in her throat.

Whatever she had been expecting to find in the oves, this was not it. He looked human. And stunningly beautiful. And his green eyes were fixed on her face so strangely that Desada couldn't remember what she should do.

With a soft frown, he opened his mouth to speak. Suddenly, a blade was on his neck.

"Don't move," Allard said coldly. He stood behind the beautiful oaf, his sword angled over the shoulder to slice his neck with ease, the moment he needed to.

The large being's eyes widened and then another voice spoke.

"You should rethink that sword."

The three of them turned as one to find another oaf standing and watching them, identical to the first, a throwing knife in each hand.

Instinct flew back into Desada instantly and before there was room for thought, she was standing to her full and unimpressive height, an arrow poised over her fist.

The new oaf shot a calm glance at the arrow she had pointing at him.

"Without harming my brother, I can kill your friend before you've so much as pulled that little string back," he said smoothly.

"And I can kill you before you move."

They stood in silence, muscles tense, blood pounding in Desada's ears.

"You look like Nemir."

Startled, Desada shot the first oaf a glance, keeping her bow pointing at the other.

"What?" she demanded. "What about Nemir? Where is he?"

Her voice sounded shrill. She took a breath, trying to remain calm. Maybe they could somehow force these two to set him free.

"He's gone."

Desada's heart skidded painfully into her ribs.

"What?" she asked.

Without thinking, she dropped the bow and looked up at the oaf before her.

"Desada!" Prince Allard hissed.

She stepped forward, pushing the prince's arm away from the oaf's neck. Tears were already stinging her eyes.

"He's dead?" she demanded.

The oaf's eyes widened.

"No," he corrected at once. "At least I don't think so."

Giving up, Prince Allard came around with a grumble, tugging her away.

She yanked her arm out of his grasp, never looking away from the oaf's green eyes.

"What is that supposed to mean?" she demanded.

"He's not in the camp anymore."

She looked at the other as he strode up next to his twin, dropping an arm casually over his shoulders.

"If you're here to rescue the boy, you're a little late," he said. "He's already been rescued."

Both of the humans gaped.

"By who?"

They glanced at each other.

"Soluc, our brother," they said together.

"But we don't have the time to stand and chat, unfortunately."

The twins moved to walk by, but Desada reached out, grabbing the first's wrist at the last moment.

"Will you tell us where he is?" she asked hopefully. "I can't go home without him. I *won't*."

They exchanged another glance.

"Um, Desada," Prince Allard suddenly interjected. He tugged on her arm, attempting to pull her away but she brushed him off, not really noticing.

"Are you really that gifted with the bow?" the second brother asked.

Desada simply nodded.

He sighed.

"From what we've learned, both of our brothers are in danger. They both may have a better chance of surviving if you help us stop Lenroy."

"Who?" Allard asked.

"Our other brother," they said together.

***

Nemir stretched his toes out, clenching and unclenching them as he tested the tug of skin on his fresh wound.

It burned more than anything he'd felt before, but it wasn't *so* bad that he couldn't stop crying.

He sniffled and poked the skin around it.

"Stop touching it," Soluc ordered.

Nemir shot him an annoyed glare, but was distracted when the ogre pulled the skins from around his waist, exposing himself.

He ripped a strip off of it, his biceps flexing as he tore it in two and then knelt down, next to Nemir.

"What are you doing?" Nemir demanded, cringing away.

Soluc sighed.

"I'm going to make us other stuff to wear with that," he indicated the boar lying dead several feet off. "So that I can fix you up."

Soluc pulled Nemir's leg out gently, his fingers lingering on his bare thigh.

Nemir looked up, meeting his gaze. He flushed and looked away, quickly.

"You should really pee on this."

Nemir's jaw dropped open.

"What?!" he demanded.

"The river is the opposite direction," Soluc pointed out. "There's no water in this area."

Nemir's lips flapped around aimlessly, searching for words.

Soluc chuckled.

"Somehow, I didn't think you'd be into that idea."

He wrapped the fur around the wound tightly. It had stopped bleeding, but every time he moved too suddenly, blood still oozed from its depths.

He gasped as Soluc tied it off, and shut his eyes, waiting for the pain to subside.

When he opened his eyes again, Soluc was hoisting the boar's corpse gratefully out of Nemir's sight.

He smiled and leaned back. The forest was a lot less intimidating when he wasn't alone. In the short while that Soluc had been off killing the thing, Nemir had been sure that a wild beast would appear out of nowhere, drawn by the scent of his blood.

Luckily, the only beast who felt drawn to him in any way was Soluc himself. And that was most likely out of obligation.

Back at the camp, when Soluc had pushed those other ogres apart and looked down at Nemir, he had been certain that he'd never seen a more beautiful sight. Now, with his life safely secured however, reality slammed back into him harder with each step that they took.

And then there was the marriage thing.

The sound of skin ripping from muscle impeded Nemir's thoughts. He swallowed hard, glad that he had already emptied his stomach of its miniscule contents earlier.

"Soluc," he called. "How long will it be until we eat?"

There was a lengthy pause.

"Are you hungry now?" Soluc called over.

Nemir rolled his eyes. He'd been hungry since he'd first woken up at the camp *days* ago.

"I'm starving."

The disturbing noises continued.

"It won't be long then," he called.

Nemir looked up at the sky, wondering if he should time his new—husband. Ugh. Even in his head it was impossibly hard to think.

His blood bubbled furiously at the thought. It had been so quick that night. They had barely said a few words. All they'd done was burn some hair and toss dust in his face.

He scowled and looked up, attempting to find the exact position of the sun through the thick, rustling, leaves.

Sure, it may not be entirely Soluc's fault, but he was the one who'd got Nemir into this entire mess and he sure as hell was going to suffer for it.

Nemir didn't realize that he'd dozed off until Soluc was gently lifting him from his spot at the base of the tree he'd planted himself at.

Startled, Nemir stiffened, grabbing onto Soluc's shoulder.

"You didn't look very comfortable there," Soluc said in explanation and knelt down into the grass, settling before a small fire with Nemir in his lap.

Nemir attempted to push out of Soluc's embrace, but his leg cried out in protest and he just slumped against his hard chest instead.

Attempting to ignore the fact that they were both very naked, and pressed together, he fixed his eyes on the meat sizzling on a makeshift spit.

Nemir looked up at the sky, suddenly remembering his decision to complain as much as he saw necessary. It was getting late into the evening, everything beginning to dim, but it had only been about an hour since he'd slept. Unfortunately, he couldn't fault the guy for skinning an animal, cutting up its meat, starting a decent fire and beginning to cook in that amount of time.

Nemir scowled. Soluc was lucky, this time.

"How does your leg feel?" Soluc asked.

Nemir shrugged.

"Fine," he said.

Why was the brute so darn *comfortable*?

"What about your head?"

He kissed the back of Nemir's head, in just the spot that he had been struck by that rock.

He reached a hand up, gingerly touching the spot. There was a bump there now, but Nemir only felt it when it was touched.

"It's okay," he said.

Had Soluc even been there for that? That had happened right at the start, while he'd still been standing in the circle and everyone was trying to decide how best to finish him.

He shuddered and Soluc tightening his warm embrace, his arms slipping around Nemir's waist.

"What about your toes?" he asked. He pressed his soft lips to Nemir's cheek, momentarily distracting him.

Nemir frowned.

"What about them?"

"Didn't someone step on them?" Soluc asked, nipping his ear.

Nemir pulled away with a frown. Rather than complain about the teeth being used on him, he raked his brain over the events. Had someone stepped on him?

His eyes widened. Yes. For a split second he'd been pinned in place by someone's large foot landing on his amid the chaos.

He looked up at Soluc.

"How do you know about that?" he demanded.

Soluc smiled.

"We're married now," he said softly. "I could feel it."

He leaned in to kiss Nemir on the lips this time, but Nemir pulled away.

What was he doing? What was he letting *happen* here?

He struggled out of Soluc's hold, ignoring his protesting muscles and realized the absurdity of sitting naked in someone's lap. Someone who wasn't even *human. A*nd whether they were married or not, was beside the point.

He hadn't had a choice in any of this.

Trembling, Nemir looked up, meeting the ogre's deep, expressive eyes. They were confused now, but above all, weary.

"Tell me," he started. "The other day—."

He swallowed hard and forced himself on.

"When we—"

"Made love," Soluc supplied.

Nemir nodded.

"Yeah," he said. "Was that because—was it because of the spell?"

Soluc didn't answer for a long time, but his silence was answer enough.

"It makes you want each other," he finally said. "Until after it's been consummated."

Nemir shut his eyes, an array of emotions rushing through his veins. The most prominent of which, was relief.

This really wasn't his fault. He hadn't just given himself away, without any thought, to someone that wasn't human. To someone that was a male and an ogre.

It explained everything. His draw to Soluc, coupled with his aversion. The aversion had been real, the draw had been a spell.

A hand gripped his.

"Nemir."

He opened his eyes, meeting Soluc's intense stare.

It wasn't his fault, either. He'd felt it, just the way Nemir had. Nemir's heart skipped.

"The spell pushed us both," Soluc said. Nemir nodded, a smile lifting his lips.

Soluc leaned forward. "But it's not anymore," he said, "and I still want you."

Nemir started.

"What?" he asked. "But you don't have to. You're an ogre—"

"I'm not," Soluc said, smiling. "I'm an oaf."

Nemir sighed.

"Fine, and I'm a human—"

Soluc touched a finger to his lips, silencing him.

"I don't care," he said.

He leaned forward, closing the distance between them swiftly, and pressing their lips together.

An explosion of nerves swamped the pit of Nemir's stomach. As they drew apart, he took a shaking breath.

"Are you sure that the spell's not still working?" he asked.

Soluc just smiled and kissed him again.

CHAPTER TWELVE

The cool night air made it impossible to sleep. Nemir inched a little bit closer to the dimming fire, but it didn't help much. The earth was freezing against his skin.

"You're being ridiculous," Soluc said, somewhat impatiently.

Nemir shut his eyes, pretending to be sleeping.

"You *know* that if we sleep against each other, we'll be warmer."

Nemir continued to feign sleep until Soluc sighed heavily.

"Do you want more firewood then?" he asked.

After a brief pause, Nemir nodded.

He rolled over, watching Soluc's back disappear into the darkness.

It was a wonder he did it with so little hesitation. Even with the light of the fire, the gentle creaks and noises around them, put Nemir on edge.

Not to mention that his head was starting to really hurt. Whether it was because of the knock it had received earlier today, or the stress of the whole situation, he was unsure. Not that it mattered at this point.

Nemir pressed the back of his skull to the cold ground, relishing the slow numbing of pain.

He wondered if he could get his cut leg against it too.

After a moment of twisting unsuccessfully, he opened his eyes with a sigh and found Soluc staring down at him, a bundle of sticks in his arms.

Nemir sat up with a start, his brain bouncing around painfully in his skull.

Soluc raised a brow, an amused smile on his lips.

"What are you doing?" he asked.

Luckily, in the dark, Nemir doubted that his blush was very visible.

"It's none of your business," he retorted.

The haughty tone was usually enough for people to stop bothering him.

Soluc walked up to his side and knelt down silently. He began to methodically place the wood into the fire.

"Does your leg hurt?" he asked casually.

Nemir scowled at his back.

"I said it's none of your business."

Soluc dropped the last of the wood into the fire and watched for a moment as it began to flare up. He turned to look at Nemir slowly, his eyes narrowed.

He reached out to Nemir, taking his face gently in both hands.

"I already told you that I could feel it, or did you not believe me?"

Nemir swallowed.

He opened his mouth to speak, but all words left him as he was pushed flat to the ground.

"What are you doing?" he demanded. Why was his voice trembling so hard?

Soluc smiled down at him.

"There's nothing much we can do about your wounds for now, but I can definitely try to distract you from them."

Nemir's eyes widened.

"No," he said at once.

He tried to push himself up, but a strong hand held him down.

"I don't want to do—*that*—again," Nemir said. His voice sounded panicked, even to his own ears.

"Don't worry," Soluc said. He dropped his head down, kissing Nemir's stomach, softly. A thrill of desire coursed through Nemir's body.

He shut his eyes. No. This couldn't happen. Not while he wasn't being pushed by outside forces.

Soluc ran his hands along Nemir's thighs, carefully avoiding his bound injury. His lips traced the path.

All Nemir had to do was say no, and he was sure that Soluc would stop. He had been carrying out every one of Nemir's orders all day.

Nemir opened his mouth, but only a soft gasp escaped as Soluc licked along his length.

His tongue lapped against him and then suddenly Nemir was completely engulfed in Soluc's deep, hot mouth.

Nemir dropped his head back, with a cry.

He tried to lift up to watch, but as Soluc began to suck, all he could do was throw himself back, arching into the wet mouth, straining against the hands rubbing circles against his hips.

Sensing his nearness, Soluc's soft lips tightened around him, sucking him harder until the familiar array of lights exploded before Nemir's eyes.

He strained against Soluc's mouth, shaking as every last drop he had to offer, spilled into his mouth.

As the roaring of blood through his ears began to quiet, Nemir realized that his gasps were all that could be heard, as he strained for air.

Soluc licked the last drops up, and began to trail kisses along his length as he softened.

Nemir shut his eyes, choosing to avoid watching the action. Even though he was tired from his release, it still felt good. He didn't really want Soluc to stop kissing and touching him.

Belatedly, he unclenched his fingers from their tangled mess in Soluc's long hair and pulled his hands up to his face, covering it.

Soluc was right about one thing; if Nemir was still in pain, he couldn't feel it, and he didn't care to.

Soluc adjusted himself against Nemir, tracing his warm hands comfortably over him.

Nemir shuddered and rolled away.

There was a long silence, filled only with Nemir's uneven breaths.

"What's wrong?" Soluc finally asked.

The confused tone of his voice made Nemir's eyes sting with tears.

This wasn't Soluc's fault, not really, but he sure as hell wasn't helping matters.

"What am I supposed to do?" Nemir asked softly. "Go live with you and all the other ogres that want to skin me just for fun?"

He rolled over, meeting Soluc's troubled frown with his own.

"You keep saying that," Soluc said uneasily. "We aren't ogres. We're oves."

Nemir sighed.

"What's the difference?"

Soluc's frown deepened, but he didn't answer the question.

"We can work something out," he said.

"Like what?" Nemir asked. "Would you want to come home with me, meet my family and live in a palace on the other side of the sea?"

Soluc shut his eyes and shook his head softly.

Nemir bit his lip.

"It doesn't matter," Nemir whispered. "They would never accept you."

Soluc opened his eyes, fixing them on Nemir.

"Why not?" he asked.

Despite everything, Nemir laughed.

"Well first of all, you had me kidnapped and almost killed."

"That was an accident." He gripped Nemir's hand fiercely. "And you know I wouldn't have let you get hurt."

With a bitter smile, Nemir looked down pointedly at his bound leg. Soluc's grip tightened.

"I know," he said. "But it'll never happen again. Not while I'm still living."

Nemir's heart skipped. He looked away.

"It doesn't matter," he said. "You're still not human and above all else, you're still a *male*."

Soluc frowned.

"What's wrong with that?" he asked.

Nemir smiled, cheerlessly. This *definitely* wasn't Soluc's fault then.

"Human's don't do that," he said simply.

Soluc's frown deepened.

With a sigh, Nemir rolled onto his back, staring up at the trees. It was a fairly nice night. He bet that if they were in an open space, they would be staring at the stars right now.

"Can it be reversed?"

"What?" Soluc asked.

"The—*marriage*."

He had to whisper the word.

"I don't know," Soluc answered. "I've never heard of anyone doing that before."

"Do you know of anyone who *would* know?"

Soluc thought for a moment.

"I suppose the elves would know," he said slowly. "But I doubt they would bother telling us."

"Why not?" Nemir asked. "You—*oves*—are half elf, aren't you?"

Soluc chuckled, darkly.

"Yes and as you're so quick to point out, we're also half *ogre*. That's too much of a disgrace for most elves to face."

So that was that? They were stuck together?

Acting as though the conversation was over, Soluc scooted closer, closing the short distance between them and snuggling against Nemir's side.

Evidently, he was right, because combined with Soluc's warm embrace, the heat and flickering of the fire put him to sleep in an instant.

***

Pain dragged Nemir from the depths of sleep. He opened his eyes, holding back a moan and squeezed them shut again when he realized that he was facing a sculpted chest.

He listened to the steady sound of Soluc's breathing as it ruffled his hair, and peeked to make sure that he was sleeping.

Satisfied, Nemir eased himself as gently as he could from the embrace, his leg stinging more than ever.

He dragged himself next to the fire, hoping that with the dim embers and lightening sky, he would be able to see.

Carefully, he untied the binding, prying it away. He stopped immediately, realizing that his flesh had begun to heal around the fur.

Shoot. He needed to get it off, at once.

For the better part of an hour, Nemir attempted to pull and pry the thing off, but he couldn't, without pulling off half of his skin with it. The worst parts were where the fur had actually managed to snake under the bindings, and fuse with his skin.

Finally, Nemir just wrapped the whole thing up again, and collapsed against the damp grass.

He lay still for a while, waiting for the pain to ebb away. Despite himself, Nemir found himself thinking of the previous night. The conversation replayed in his mind, and more importantly, so did the events proceeding the conversation.

It was almost like a reflex, Nemir reflected. From now on, when he wanted to be distracted from pain, he wondered whether he would always think of soft hair, warm lips, and strong hands.

He opened his eyes, realizing the direction that his memories were leading him.

Soluc slept on, unaware of Nemir's unrest. He didn't seem too disturbed by the fact that they were stuck with one another. The only logical reason for that was, he didn't realize how much Nemir would get in the way of his life.

It was a wonder that the large ogre—*oaf* was not already cursing his existence, for uprooting him from his gang.

Nemir gazed at Soluc with a sudden surge of guilt. He wasn't the only one who was losing everything because of this.

With a grim clenching of his jaw, Nemir pushed up to his feet. He bit his lip, harder than ever, to keep from making any noises and looked around. It wasn't long until morning and Soluc, no doubt, would awaken with the sun.

He had to keep quiet.

Nemir crept through the soft grass, remembering the way that Allard had eased his way through the very same forest, before any of this had happened.

Nemir knew it was crazy. He would probably starve before he got out, but he knew which way was north, at least, and he would continue on south until he was back amongst the humans again.

His heart was pounding with excitement as he remembered his bed back at the palace. The thought propelled him on. He would get out of these god forsaken trees, eating any berries and vegetation that he thought would be safe. Once he was dressed, he could put this whole nightmare behind him. And, he amended, so could Soluc.

Thinking of Soluc made his heart skip uncomfortably against his ribs.

Nemir sighed. There was no point in that. The whole—*thing*—that he'd had with Soluc was over now, whatever it was.

The thought made him feel a little nauseous.

Was that the marriage bind affecting him?

If it was, it could just go away. If they forgot each other now, Nemir doubted a little twinge every now and then when he hurt himself, would be much of a bother. What else were they supposed to do? Force a bunch of elves to reverse the ceremony for them?

He snorted.

Even in his head, it sounded unlikely.

Something creaked loudly behind him and Nemir spun around abruptly, his heart jumping into his throat.

His thigh burned from the effort and he looked down, finding blood oozing free from beneath the bindings.

"Darn it," he cursed.

He took a deep breath to ease the pain.

Why did it smell like firewood here? He was too far from the oves' camp to smell it and the embers that he had just left behind, were far too diminished to emit such a strong odor.

A stillness over took Nemir, settling over him as he looked into the dark woods.

It was a belated thought… but his blood *would* draw hungry animals from the trees. He knew that much about the wild, at least, but these woods did not seem to be dangerous. All the food they'd eaten had come from relatively harmless animals, aside from the boar.

He placed a palm against his pounding heart, attempting to ease it, but a loud rushing noise made it pound even harder.

He swung around at the sound, all of the hairs rising on his arms.

Something was close. Very close.

He had never heard a noise like that. Wait, hadn't he heard about beasts in the Tasnian wilds before? Things like manticores and basilisks and—

He should run.

Fire blazed, just at the corner of Nemir's vision.

Run! He told himself, but his legs were frozen in place.

Snapping twigs, the rustle of leaves and underbrush and an unidentifiable *thumping* alerted him that the creature was coming closer.

Finally, Nemir's limbs remembered how to work and he stumbled backwards, away from the noises, falling onto his back and scuffling back even farther as the creature emerged.

It had a face that Nemir had only seen before in paintings; a large mouth, glistening fangs and a mane that flowed out about it. A lions head on the more familiar body of a goat. Large talon-like ridges, rose from its back, leading into its long and serpentine tale.

Its eyes fixed coldly on Nemir and the tail whipped out behind it, *thwacking* into the bark of a tree and sending wood splintering from the spot.

A chimera.

The beast opened its mouth and Nemir knew what would follow. A blast of fire to cook him for lunch.

Nemir's whole life played before his eyes in an instant and unfortunately, it was a very short and uninteresting life. Until he had been forced to visit Tasnia, representing his home country, he had barely ever travelled, and until he had been kidnapped and forced to marry a male, half-ogre he had never felt anything more threatening than mild boredom. In the past few days, he'd felt crippling fear on a number of levels, and he'd felt other things too, the most terrifying of which were all to do with Soluc.

And he had left Soluc lying asleep and unaware and hadn't said a word about what he was feeling, because he hadn't thought it was worth it.

Would Soluc feel it, when he was burned to ashes?

The fire billowed from the chimera's lips on a snarl, as though in slow motion. The heat of it touched Nemir's face, and then suddenly, its head was knocked hard aside with the heavy swing of a club.

The thing staggered to the side. It shook out its head and turned its intense gaze on Soluc.

With a frightening swiftness, Soluc swung the branch out again, bringing it down with all of his weight into the creature's skull.

A heavy *crack* echoed through the trees around them and the thing collapsed to the ground, its heavy tail whipping out wildly in its last moments of life.

"Soluc!" Nemir cried, but it was too late. The strong limb struck Soluc's back. Blood sprayed the tree behind him and he fell to his knees.

A crippling pain shot through Nemir's back.

He cried out.

Convulsing in pain, his whole body shuddering, Nemir bit down on his lip, until finally, the pain subsided as though it was never there.

He reached a hand tenderly to his back, realizing that he was fine. With a gasp, he sat up, his eyes landing on Soluc's unconscious and bloodied form.

CHAPTER THIRTEEN

Soluc woke up to a stinging pain in his leg. He opened his eyes and instinctively looked down at the limb in question until the pain suddenly subsided. It was Nemir. Which was odd, because his leg was already injured. Why was it stinging him again?

He sat up with a start, realizing that the wound must have split open once again.

Only a brief glance was needed to know that Nemir was gone and a twisting in the pit of Soluc's stomach, told him that he wasn't just off taking a leak.

His muscles and joints cracked indignantly as he jumped to his feet, but he ignored his body as he searched around the clearing.

A set of faint but fresh footprints had him running after Nemir.

Didn't humans know how stupid it was to be alone in the wild? Especially in these parts.

Soluc smelled the telltale burning of wood, first. His arm reached out instinctively to grab at the larges fallen branch within his grasp, and he continued on. Knowing Nemir's luck, he was about to be eaten–and with the end of his life, would come Soluc's as well. Lenroy would get what he wanted at last.

Finally, Soluc saw the chimera. Its mouth opened to feed, and Nemir stood, stunned, before it. He could feel Nemir's eyes on him as he cracked through the animal's skull, could hear him screaming in pain as the sharp spikes of its tale raked across Soluc's back.

"Idiot," Soluc muttered.

"What?" Nemir asked.

Soluc ignored him.

"Soluc," Nemir whispered softly. He touched a hand to his face and it felt cool and so sweet. "Are you awake?"

Soluc opened his eyes reluctantly, and was met with a view of dangerously dark eyes gazing down at him.

"Nemir," he said.

His voice came out rough and unused. Why was he so groggy? He attempted to roll over, but a searing pain ravaged his body at the movement.

"Don't," Nemir said, sternly.

He reached out a hand and placed it comfortingly on Soluc's shoulder, while the pain began to subside.

It didn't disappear completely, but continued on in an agonizing, pounding rhythm, pumping through his body.

"Are you hungry?" Nemir asked, gently.

Soluc shook his head. He couldn't even begin to think of food. He couldn't think of anything but the pain. The chimera's tail must have poisoned him, or else cut right into his spine. He couldn't imagine anything else that would hurt so much.

"How long has it been?" he bit out.

"A day," Nemir said.

A day? It was morning again, judging by what Soluc could see. He was lying on his side, his head resting on the skins he had prepared for Nemir's clothing. He could feel the heat of a fire warming him softly.

How had Nemir managed to move Soluc here to care for him? He was so small. It must have been an effort to do all of this.

Suddenly, he could think of something that would make him feel better, something that would take away at least a little of the pain.

"Come here," he whispered.

Nemir didn't answer for a moment and then, silently, he lay down and scooted against Soluc's chest.

Up close, Soluc could see the red bags under his eyes. He hadn't slept a wink, had he?

"I'm sorry," Nemir whispered, shutting his eyes. He reached up an arm, wrapping it around Soluc's back while expertly avoiding his wound.

Soluc kissed his forehead in reply.

Much as the boy was an idiot, Soluc was still glad that he had made it in time to save him. Even without the marriage bind, he doubted that he ever would have let him die.

"Soluc," Nemir whispered, seriously. "I think we should go to the elves."

Reversing their marriage… It was the only logical choice left, so Soluc was surprised by just how much those words upset him.

Great. Now he had plenty to think of besides the pain.

***

Allard was more than just a dashingly handsome swordsman and expert hunter. He was a prince with the class, sense of humor, and intelligence, to make an entire kingdom fall to his feet in adoration. Although, out here, it seemed like he was just an unnecessary extra, moments from blending into the trees.

"I suggest we take the other route around the swamp," he said for the third time, albeit much more loudly this time.

"I don't think we can handle a trip through the swamps," Desada said as though he hadn't spoken.

The other two nodded thoughtfully.

"I still think taking the eastern route would be best," Memet said.

Allard didn't often lose his temper, but he was beginning to wonder why the heck he was even here.

"I was under the impression that this was *my* rescue mission, which *you*," he poked a finger roughly into Desada's shoulder, "decided to come along for, and then you two decided to take over."

Desada shot a hot glare at him, but to his surprise, Tuboy held back a smile and Memet laughed out right.

"What?!" he snapped furiously. "This isn't funny! Why are you all acting like I don't even exist? I'm a prince! My opinion is worth at *least* as much as yours are!"

Memet's grin widened.

"Not out here it isn't," he said. "Plus, the ogres live to the West."

Allard scowled. He knew it made his forehead do that creasing-thing that he hated, but at the moment, he could care less.

"They can't be worse than you lot," he muttered.

The twins laughed and even Desada giggled. Allard huffed. Why was it that his jokes were never well received, unless they were accidental?

"Trust us," Tuboy said. "We are nowhere *near* as bad as the Ogres."

He glanced at Memet.

"I guess it would be safe to say that we take after our Elvin heritage the most."

Memet grinned and smacked his brother roughly on the shoulder.

"Don't let any elves hear you say that."

Allard found that hard to believe, but decided to let it go in favor of his other concern.

"How do we even know that they're all headed that way?" he asked. "What if we take the long way to the elves, and then instead of beating them there, we find out that they're already out of the forest with that brother of yours on their trail?"

To Allard's pleasure, their amused expressions all dropped from their faces.

"It's true," Desada said. It was about time. She was human and therefore supposed to take his side. "We can't leave their trail. Lenroy might catch up to them while we take the long way."

Tuboy shook his head.

"I know my brothers," he said. "Lenroy's not very good at tracking." He looked at Allard pointedly. "The fact that he took the wrong prince, and took so long to get him in the first place, is proof enough of that."

Tuboy shut his eyes, deep in thought.

"Judging by the tracks, it should take him a few more days to catch them."

Allard glared up at the twins. It was no secret that he hated the fact that they had teamed up together, but it made sense in a way. What still *didn't* make sense to him though, was the rest of the situation.

"I don't get it," he said. "Why is Soluc *protecting* Nemir? Believe me, I've been hunting with him. He's probably only slowing your brother down."

The twins exchanged a heavy look that had Allard's eyes narrowing.

He exchanged his own look with Desada and as one they turned on the oves.

"What are you not telling us?" Desada demanded.

The touch of a smile lifted Memet's lips, but it looked more sinister than anything. Especially with Tuboy frowning at his side.

"They were lovers," he said.

The human's stared up at their companions blankly.

"Do you humans have a different word for it or something?" Memet asked.

"What?!" Desada and Allard demanded together.

"Oh, it was completely consensual of course, don't worry."

Allard was fairly sure his eyes were about to pop out of his skull from the shock. *Consensual*? Allard hadn't really thought of it being anything else until he said *that*. Of course. How could Nemir—sweet naïve Nemir—consensually sleep with a half ogre?

"Don't worry?!" he demanded.

Memet patted him on the head fondly.

"There's something cute about you, when you're angry," he said.

Allard spluttered for a moment, an angry flush rising to his cheeks, a frown gluing his brows together.

He honestly hadn't even considered dangers like *that*.

He had let Nemir down in the worst way and even if he didn't know the boy very well, he still liked him. Quite a lot, actually. He was one of the first people who had been blatantly honest with Allard. And although he was just realizing now that he didn't always like people's honest reactions to him, he still appreciated Nemir.

And now…

He looked up at the oves. How had he come to be so at ease with them? They were still animals. Probably closer in thought process to the beasts of the forest than they were to him. He looked at Desada. Her face was still a mask of shock. Her eyes were wide and confused. She was beautiful as always.

And Allard had allowed her to travel with these beasts all this time.

"I have an idea," he said.

His voice sounded relatively normal to him, but it drew everyone's eyes to him at once.

"We'll split up," he said. "We'll go the short way, you take the safe way."

Not waiting for a reply, he grabbed Desada's hand and pulled her away.

Tuboy stepped in front of him, clearly alarmed.

"That's not a good idea," he said.

"Get out of the way," Allard said.

"There are more dangers out there than just the ogres, even if you manage to avoid them," Memet said, joining his brother. "This is the largest forest in all of Tasnia. It stretches from the north to the south and houses more creatures than there are humans in all of this land."

"Yes, and your brother is one of those creatures," Allard said. "Don't try to stop us."

"Allard," Desada whispered. Clearly, the oaf's warning was weighing on her. "What are you doing?"

He glanced her.

"Think about what they did to your brother," he hissed. "Do you really want to stick with more oves?"

She frowned but didn't say anything.

Allard's frown firmly in place, he continued to pull her along. This journey was going to take a serious toll on the speed of his aging.

***

Soluc was an oaf driven by instincts. That's why he did so well with most things and that's how he had come to lead this escapade.

Instinct had told him to take the leadership role, instinct had told him not to trust Lenroy to capture the prince, and the strongest instinct of all, had told him to keep Nemir alive. Okay, maybe that last one was a little more than just instinct.

He had ignored his instinct when it came to Lenroy and here he was in the middle of a dangerous forest with only a tiny human and a wrenching pain in his body.

But his instinct was forcing him to open his eyes now.

Soluc lay for a moment in the near morning light, wondering why he was awake. He blinked sleepily, Nemir's soft curls tickling his cheeks.

The pain was still there, but seemed to be easing slightly. If it weren't for his size, he doubted that he would have survived the chimera's strike.

Thankfully, he'd made it there when he had.

His arms tightened around Nemir and to his surprise the human snuggled into him with a contented sigh.

It was the first time he'd seemed remotely relaxed with Soluc.

Soluc pressed his face into the dark curls and his stomach twisted uncomfortably.

Soluc opened his eyes again.

He lifted his head, squeezing his eyes shut as his body screamed for him to rest again. Finally, he opened his eyes and looked around.

He could see no one. In fact, he was sure that they were alone. But still, something was making his body itch to get up and begin their journey again.

"Nemir," he whispered softly.

Nemir sighed in response.

Soluc looked down at him, and unable to help himself, he pressed his lips to the prince's tiny ear.

Again, Nemir sighed.

"Nemir," he whispered against it. "Wake up."

"I'm awake," he muttered sleepily.

A moment later he was snoring softly and Soluc had to hold back a laugh.

Soluc bent his head down over him, allowing his lips to rake over the softly parted mouth below him. Nemir was a mystery to the oaf. He was young, rather adorable, completely inexperienced with life, from what Soluc could tell, and he was inexplicably unhappy about the fact that he enjoyed Soluc's touch as thoroughly as he did.

Proving his point, Nemir sighed softly against his lips, encouraging Soluc to press down into him. He had never tasted anything so sweet.

Soluc dipped his tongue into the receiving mouth. Nemir didn't need any further encouragement. His lips drifted apart welcomingly, their tongues meeting and languidly massaging against each other.

All other thoughts and distractions vanished from Soluc's mind.

His eyes drifted open ever so slightly. Soluc froze, realizing that two onyx orbs were now watching him.

He pulled back as everything around him came slowly back into focus; the urgency in the air around him, the pain coursing through his back, the chilly morning air.

Nemir gazed up at him with a securely closed off expression. Nothing that he was thinking showed through, but the blankness was more than enough to make Soluc's gut twist uncomfortably.

"Well this is frustrating," he murmured.

Nemir looked away.

"Are we going to have sex again?" he asked.

The touch of unease in his voice had the complete opposite effect on Soluc's body than love making with the human normally would have.

"No," he said. With a grimace, he pushed himself up and away from the boy, trying to ignore the shiver that ran through him at the loss of bodily contact.

Soluc straightened himself, eliciting a sharp hiss of pain.

Nemir was at his side in an instant, holding him steady.

"You should stay down," he said.

Surprised by the complete turnaround, Soluc looked at him closely.

Nemir wore the same closely guarded expression as before, but a touch of worry lined his eyes, along with something else. Knowing Nemir wouldn't like it, Soluc gripped the boy's chin anyway, holding his small face steady. Nemir shifted uncomfortably for a moment and then simply looked away, his brow creased unhappily.

Soluc frowned. He didn't often see this expression amongst his people. He wasn't use to such an obvious display of guilt.

"This isn't your fault," he said.

Okay, maybe it was a little, but it didn't matter anymore.

Nemir yanked his face free, his cheeks turning that adorable pink color.

"You should be resting," he said it angrily, but his voice was shaking.

Soluc smiled.

"We don't have the time," he said. "Someone's following us."

Startled, Nemir shot a heavy look into the trees around them as though expecting the culprit to be standing just out of sight, waiting for them to finish their conversation.

Finally, he fixed those piercing black eyes back on Soluc.

"How do you know?" he demanded.

Soluc frowned.

"I don't know," he said uncomfortably. "I can just sense it."

Nemir's doubtful gaze thickened, but then, to Soluc's surprise, he bent to retrieve their bundle of fresh furs. As a last thought, he tossed some dirt onto their long diminished fire and looked up at Soluc.

"So which way are we going then?" he asked.

Soluc swallowed. It was a little silly how much Nemir's blind trust warmed him, but he couldn't help the feeling.

"West," he said. His voice came out soft and drenched with emotion. He cleared his throat, glad that only Nemir had the displeasure of hearing him like this. "It's the fastest way to get to the elves while avoiding the swamp."

Nemir nodded and looked up at the sky, clearly trying to figure out which way west would be.

Soluc smiled softly.

"It's this way," he said.

He reached out a hand. Nemir looked at it and then, after a long moment, he took it in his own.

Soluc swallowed. He didn't know whether it was their bond that was making him feel this way. He didn't care.

Squeezing Nemir's soft hand gently in his own, they began to walk.

CHAPTER FOURTEEN

Soluc knew something was wrong almost at once. Nemir was limping worse than before. As the pain in his back turned into a dull burn and stopped distracting him, Soluc realized it.

The little human had his head bowed, his teeth grit in obvious pain, but he didn't make a sound, choosing instead to grip Soluc's hand in an iron clasp. His knuckles turned white and after a while, his other hand came up, wrapping around Soluc's biceps for added support.

"How's your leg?" Soluc asked unnecessarily.

Nemir didn't respond.

Finally, Soluc came to a stop.

Nemir stopped walking and looked up at Soluc, dazed.

"Huh?" he asked.

With an impatient growl, Soluc dropped to his knees, ignoring his own pain, and began to untie Nemir's binding.

Nemir's entire body stiffened at once.

"Don't pull it," he begged.

Surprised, it was only a moment before Soluc realized why he was so worried.

The entire wound had fused onto the fur around it and from the little Soluc could see, it was already badly infected.

Soluc cursed.

"Why didn't you tell me?" he demanded.

"I could have told you," Nemir said defiantly. "But you wouldn't have heard, considering that you were unconscious."

Soluc scowled. He hated being wrong. He shouldn't have let that damn chimera touch him. He knew about the tails. He had been careless.

He looked up at Nemir and knew by the way that the boy shrank away that he had that same fierce expression in his eyes. It was the one that had lead everyone to fear him, even though he rarely followed through on his gruesome promises.

Soluc had seen wounds like this one before. One in particular, and the recipient had left it untreated. More accurately, no one had known *how* to treat it. She had gotten a fever first and then the wound had festered. Her presence was filled with the smell of rot. By the time anyone knew what to do, it had spread through her system, poisoning her blood. Within days they were burying a cold body. Two in fact, her and her husband both.

Soluc reached up, roughly pulling the furs off of Nemir's shoulder where they rested.

He flinched hard, but Soluc ignored that.

He laid them down flat on the ground, and eyed Nemir's hips, judging the size. Nemir squirmed.

"What are you doing?" he demanded.

Ignoring him, Soluc gripped an uneven edge and ripped the thing in two.

The piece was narrow and long, but probably just right for Nemir's svelte form.

He tugged him close and wrapped it around his narrow hips, almost twice, before tucking it into place. Then he took the rest and pushed himself to his feet.

Nemir was staring at him; his eyes wide but a smile touched his lips.

"Thank you," he said.

Soluc stared. He had heard the food theory before but it seemed that the way to *this* boy's heart was through clothing. He wrapped the remainder around Nemir's shoulders like a scarf and ruffled his hair.

"We need to keep you warm," he said. "And at the first sign of fresh water, you're going to have to soak that thing off."

He gestured to Nemir's leg.

"Come on," he said.

He took a few steps and after a moment, looked back at Nemir.

He was standing still and looking down at the furs intently.

"What is it?" Soluc asked.

Nemir looked up at him. His eyes dipped down to his naked hips and he averted his gaze at once, his cheeks turning pink—which Soluc thought was rather silly.

"You've done a lot more than look at it," he said. "Why are you so embarrassed?"

Nemir flushed.

"That's not the point!" he snapped.

He pulled the remaining fur from his neck and tossed it at Soluc.

"Cover up," he instructed.

Soluc grinned and did as he was told. He loved it when Nemir showed his spoiled, princely side. Hey, if that was the way Nemir wanted it, then he would get it. Now Soluc would just have to take it upon himself to keep Nemir warm.

He walked back to the boy, wrapped an arm around his shoulders and began to walk.

His amusement faded quickly as they continued on their way. Every now and then, when the wound was pulled too hard, a sharp pain shot through Soluc's leg. Nemir was suffering, and Soluc's own body was protesting fiercely to all of the physical exertion.

He was sure that, given the opportunity, he would have slept for another day, at least, while the sting faded from his back and his muscles stopped screaming from the pain. Instead, he was making it worse. A lot worse.

Nemir stumbled and Soluc caught him just a moment from hitting the ground.

He grit his teeth and tugged the human up, but Nemir slipped back down promptly, in a slump.

"I can't go any farther," he gasped.

Tears were glistening in his eyes.

With a sigh, Soluc looked around them, trying to judge how far they had made it.

The trees were thinning considerably which was a good sign. The forest was more narrow and sparse around the swamp, which meant that they were reaching it now. Just beyond the swamps, before the plains, that would be where the elves were.

Normally, Soluc would avoid the area at all costs. Only once, as a small child, had he wandered too near to the Elvin lands and he had never gone too close again.

Now, for the first time, he was headed the fastest way possible into their depths.

He dropped his gaze to Nemir. He was cradling his thigh gently, gingerly trying to find a position to sit, that wouldn't hurt.

"I don't think we have the time to stop," Soluc said seriously.

Nemir looked up at him desperately, his eyes pleading. He looked exhausted and worn out. Even more than when he'd first woken up in the midst of the oves.

"I'm hungry," he said.

Soluc had to look away. Nemir's big, sad eyes were too much.

"The sooner we can get there, the sooner this will all be over," he promised.

Nemir reached up, seizing Soluc's hand and forcing him to look down at him.

"I don't think you understand," he said. "Human's eat several times a day."

He squeezed Soluc's hand.

"I feel like I'm starving to death. I'm tired and I'm hungry and it hurts to walk."

Soluc shut his eyes, wracking his mind for alternatives. He wanted desperately to smash his fists into something, but all that would do was scare the boy. Nemir scared easily, that much was undeniable.

Could they rest until the morning? The thought sent a spark of alarms through Soluc. Clearly, that would be a bad idea, but they were travelling so slowly and laboriously. How was it that whoever was following them hadn't caught up yet? Unless they were having a hard time with tracking.

A rush of cold ran through Soluc's body.

It was Lenroy.

They may not have always been the best of friends, but Soluc knew his brother. He knew him well. He couldn't track for the life of him, but he was perseverant. He never left a job unfinished.

Soluc looked down at Nemir. He was watching Soluc apprehensively. He didn't have time to find a meal for the boy, not now, but he could help with the rest, at least a little.

He knelt down next to Nemir and wordlessly, slipped an arm under his soft knees, the other going around his back.

Nemir squeaked as he was hoisted into Soluc's arms.

"What are you doing?" he demanded shrilly.

"We don't have time for food right now," Soluc said, ignoring the question. "Can you wait a few more hours?"

"Soluc, your back, put me down."

Soluc simply shook his head as he began to walk.

His tightly healing skin felt like it was close to ripping against his straining muscles, but he pushed the pain aside.

Soluc was use to pain. It was part of being an oaf. He would get hurt and pretend he was fine until it was fully healed or until it was too late. Just like his mother and that damn infected wound. That was just what they did. It was what he had grown up doing.

Nevertheless, he squeezed Nemir's slight form and stole a quick kiss before pressing on.

Before too long, the burn turned into a numbing pain and Soluc walked on in a drone. The puffs of Nemir's little breaths against his neck as he promptly fell asleep, cooled Soluc as he walked.

He blinked fuzzily, realizing that he was a split second from sleeping on his feet and looked around.

There was no way Lenroy had caught up and was biding his time, waiting for the right moment to strike Soluc down, was there? Slowing to a stop, Soluc spun in a very slow circle, his eyes scanning their surroundings. The forest was considerably thinner here. They were just on the outskirts of the swamp now.

The swamp.

Something about the place rang alarmingly in Soluc's mind. The forest was quiet here. Aside from the distant chirping of birds, there was nothing. But the forest always made noise; it breathed and creaked and moaned. Something was wrong.

His heart-rate picking up, Soluc took a careful step forward.

And the ground gave way below him.

Nemir woke up mid-fall, with a startled squeak, landing on top of Soluc who landed with a hard *crunch* into the trap.

Soluc grimaced and looked up at the entrance above them, one word rushing to the forefront of his mind.

Ogres.

"What happened?" Nemir gasped.

Finally, he looked down at Soluc and with a terrified gasp, he began to scream. He jumped more fully on top of Soluc's chest, his fingers digging into him, while Soluc's hand whipped out on reflex, smothering Nemir's voice.

Nemir gulped and swallowed and then took a shaking breath before Soluc released him.

"We're lying on bones," Nemir choked out.

Soluc nodded.

"I guessed as much."

They had to get out of here. Fast. Before the ogres arrived.

Keeping his voice calm, Soluc ordered Nemir off of him. The human gingerly got to his feet, his toes only touching the few spots of clear ground available.

He grimaced and stood still, watching as Soluc pushed to his feet.

"Soluc," he asked. "Why are we in a giant hole, filled with bones and carcasses?"

Soluc glanced around at his word and found several places where meat and sinew still clung to the bones. Most looked like animals, but two skulls he spotted, looked distinctly humanoid.

He'd screwed up. The west was riddled with ogres. Soluc knew that. He had always known that. True, it was the shorter way to the elves, and to the mountains. He had taken this route before, but he had been by himself then, and he had been careful. How could he bring Nemir here?

"Are you going to puke again?" Soluc asked, suddenly seeing the human's face.

Nemir shook his head.

"No, but how should we get out of here?"

Good question.

Soluc walked to the wall, each step crunching beneath his feet. His stomach twisted uncomfortably as he traced his hands along the smooth mud. There was no traction, no grip at all.

He had never expected such a level of detail from his animal-like ancestors. Up until now, he was certain that they were responsible only for the irrational bursts of anger and the general stupidity of the oves, but maybe that was untrue. Maybe they were responsible for the remarkable hunting skills as well.

Soluc paused in his thoughts as his hand rested against the smooth mud. There was a soft vibration running through the earth, tickling his fingers in a sporadic pattern. He frowned, pressing closer. It seemed to be getting stronger.

Or was it just getting closer?

"Soluc," Nemir suddenly hissed. "What's that sound?"

Soluc registered the sound of footsteps to match the vibrations. He looked at Nemir, and a moment later, a dark shadow covered them both.

As one, they looked up, their eyes fixing on the massive figures bowed over them. The two heads blocked out any sign of daylight aside from a dim glow. And in it, Soluc saw skin that looked as though it had been stretched too thinly over wide misshapen cheeks. Two sets of remarkably tiny eyes peered down at them in a color that Soluc had seen numerous times in the faces of his oaf counterparts; green and blue and too bright to look like an elf's or a human's.

One of the beasts began to laugh, a deep, hallow sound.

"We gots two," it said in a similar voice.

Suddenly, Nemir was against Soluc's back, clinging to him with a death-like grip, his heart pounding against Soluc's skin.

"Soluc," Nemir whispered. "It seems that I may puke, after all."

A protective flare ran through Soluc so fierce that he staggered slightly under the weight of it, shielding Nemir as he did.

The human gratefully gripped his hand.

"What are you going to do with us?" Soluc asked. It was an unnecessary question, but he needed to ask it nonetheless—even if his voice was shaking.

As though not hearing him, the ogres looked at one another.

"I wants the big one," said the second.

"No, I want it."

The first, reached into the hole so quickly that Soluc barely had time to think.

He ducked out of the way at the last instant, yanking Nemir along with him.

"Stop that," the creature muttered into the hole and its foul breath filled the air. Soluc gagged.

He ducked down as the large hand swiped at him. He was shielding Nemir, but the large hand managed to grip Soluc by the shoulder. The enormous fingers dug into his skin and *pulled*.

With a cry, Soluc was yanked into the air as though he was weightless and then dropped unceremoniously onto the hard ground between the two.

He jumped to his feet, his arms and legs posed to fight, looking from one to the other.

They were even larger from this close up. Terrifying and looming over him. Far larger than the difference between Soluc and Nemir, which led him to inappropriately wonder how an elf and ogre had ever managed to mate in the first place.

"Why d'you get it? I wants it."

They turned their disgusting maws to face one another.

"I wanna eat it. You get the small one."

"I'll have that one too."

Soluc edged toward the hole he had just been dragged from, his eyes darting down until he found Nemir, cowering in the shadows.

He was too far down. There was no way that Soluc would reach him if he tried. He bit down on his lip as the ogres began to shove each other.

Soluc knew this feeling well. It was a slow swelling of rage within him, pumping through his veins, erasing his thoughts, one by one.

But his strength would not be superior to these two enormous beasts. And if he got hurt, or worse, died, then Nemir would too.

"Hey, ogres."

They both paused and turned their combined attention to Soluc, a fist smooshed into one's face, the hair being yanked by the other.

Soluc grimaced. If the anger surging through him came from these two, then he wanted nothing to do with it.

"If you let me and my friend go free, then I'll catch you double the meat that's on our bodies."

After a long blank stare, the ogres began to laugh. The unpleasant sound itched at Soluc's ears.

"I don't need much time," he insisted. "A day at most."

Or two… and only if he worked *really* hard and fast.

The laughter didn't stop, but to Soluc's intense annoyance, it thickened.

As one, the two before him dropped their hands from one another and took a step toward Soluc. He finally understood why the earth had vibrated so at their approach. They walked as though each step was made with a struggle to lift their weight off of the ground and then dropped heavily back down to the earth.

Soluc could out run them. He could, but then—

He looked toward the deep and shadowy hole, where Nemir was crouched amongst bones and darkness. A surge of gratefulness rushed through him that he had been the one dragged out to be devoured. If it had been Nemir—

A large hand whipped out with frightening speed and gripped Soluc tightly by the arm.

Now, even if he wanted to run, he couldn't, its grip was too strong.

With a short yank, Soluc stumbled forward, his face smacking into a squishy belly, before he found his footing. The smell of rot infused his senses and he stumbled back, his back pressing into the other ogre before he realized it was even there.

They were surrounding him, and though there were only two, they seemed to encompass Soluc with their bodies.

"Don't do this," he whispered. No. Soluc didn't beg. He didn't do it but—

"I'm one of your kind."

They laughed again. The beast's grip on Soluc's arm tightened. He could feel his bones straining under the pressure and then the audible crack as it snapped.

Soluc shouted, and fell to his knees gasping, spots exploding before his eyes.

"What a sound!" one boomed.

"Soluc! Soluc!"

Nemir's cries broke through the haze of pain and Soluc squeezed his eyes shut.

He tried to focus on the sweet sound of Nemir's voice, but the rushing of blood through his ears drowned out everything but the rage.

If he died here, if Nemir died here, then it was his fault.

His body began to buzz with his rushing pulse. He knew this feeling. He knew it well. Too well. He had been trying to suppress it, but apparently instinct wouldn't just go away when one wanted it to.

With a cry, Soluc was on his feet, the ogre before him stumbled back and landed with an earth shattering *thud* onto the ground.

Soluc blinked, wondering briefly how it had happened, before seeing that his fist was still in the air, his good arm buzzing with the force of impact from punching the ogre.

An enormous hand gripped Soluc's shoulder, but he twisted out of its reach easily, spinning to face the other ogre head on.

For a long moment, it stared at Soluc and then slowly, its face twisted angrily and began to turn a frightening shade of purple.

Soluc grimaced as the thing let out a horrifying howl. It was all he could do not to clamp a hand over his ears.

He stumbled back. His back hit familiar squishy warmth.

Soluc's eyes widened and he tried to jump away, but two arms wrapped around him, tightly.

The ogre he'd knocked down had evidently gotten back up.

Soluc struggled in its grip, fighting against the monstrous strength to no avail.

"You've been a bad snack," it growled in his ear.

The other ogre strode threateningly toward them, its deep disturbing laughter now tinged with anger.

"I'm gonna like eating you," it said.

"No!" Soluc kicked and shouted and suddenly, he felt like a child in his father's grasp again. And it made no difference, what so ever. They were too strong.

The ogre finally stopped before him, and lifted a hand, clamping it around Soluc's neck.

No. He couldn't die here. Not like this. Not at the hands of two ogres.

Suddenly, the ogre's arms around him tightened even more and then, just as suddenly, they loosened. No sooner had this happened then a dozen arrows smacked into the hard flesh of the one before him.

Almost as one, the ogres fell to the ground, shaking the earth. Soluc was right behind them, landing on his knees in a coughing fit as air rushed back into his lungs.

He lay wheezing against the dirt until he had the presence of mind to lift himself enough to gauge the damage. Both ogres lay dead, pierced by so many arrows that they looked like porcupines.

All of the pain in Soluc's body chose that very moment to be known and he collapsed against the cold ground, cradling his freshly broken arm as the adrenaline faded.

"Soluc, are you okay?" he heard the trembling use of his name and opened his eyes, somehow expecting to find Nemir facing him. But Nemir was still in the hole, wasn't he?

A set of boots were staring him in the eyes instead.

Very nice boots at that. White, and impossibly clean, with what looked like silver embroidered along the sides in the patterns of vines.

Soluc lifted his eyes to the owner and found a long haired, pointed eared being—much like himself—staring down at him. Several others stepped into Soluc's line of sight.

"Quite the act of bravery you displayed," the glowing haired being said softly.

Soluc didn't know what that was supposed to mean, so he said the only thing that really made sense at the moment.

"Nemir," he whispered.

"Your friend?" the elf asked. "Don't worry, we will get him."

He made a swift gesture and two of the elves behind him went, presumably to retrieve Nemir.

Three others bent to help Soluc up.

"We should fix this arm now," one was saying.

A sharp pain stabbed Soluc's thigh where there was no wound.

He hissed.

"Watch his leg!" he shouted toward the trap.

The elf before him glanced at Nemir as he stumbled from the pit, then back at Soluc, an eyebrow raised.

"I didn't think that your kind mixed well with humans," he said. "Then again…"

Soluc ignored the direction that comment was probably headed.

"We had nothing to do with it," he said.

The elf's bright eyes narrowed.

"Someone bonded you without your consent?" he asked.

Soluc would have nodded but Nemir dropped to his side, officially distracting him.

"Are you okay?" Soluc asked.

"Obviously," Nemir snapped. He took a shuddering breath, his hands gripping Soluc's arm.

"You almost died," he whispered.

There were tears in his eyes. Of course. He would have felt Soluc's arm being crushed, his neck strangled.

He shut his eyes.

"I'm fine."

"Not quite," said one of the elves next to him, gripping Soluc's broken arm.

"Wait."

Their leader stopped the action with a hand on her shoulder and looked at Nemir significantly.

"Brace yourself," he said. "This will hurt you almost as much as it does him."

He gestured to Soluc's arm and Nemir paled.

Soluc shut his eyes.

"Don't worry," he said, trying to sound comforting. "The pain won't last long for you. It'll only be for a few seconds."

Soluc wished he could say the same for himself.

Without any more of a warning, his arm was pulled swiftly, the bone snapping back into place.

He heard Nemir's cry of pain over his own, and finally, the pain and exhaustion took over Soluc's body. He tried half-heartedly to remain conscious, but the darkness was just so inviting.

CHAPTER FIFTEEN

Desada's stomach twisted every time she thought of what had happened to Nemir. Her sweet, innocent brother, happily making love to a male? And without a ring on his finger? The thought almost made her laugh.

He had been taken advantage of. That much was clear. And as a woman who had always been taught to beware of such things, taught to take care of herself and defend herself, she wished the same care had been given to Nemir. Of course, he had been given the opportunity to learn the same things that Desada had, but no one had ever insisted on it for him, like they had for her.

She found herself dwelling on that little oversight now, filled with resentment and hoping that some of Nemir's innocence would survive this ordeal.

Then again, despite their appearances, Tuboy and Memet had their own kind of innocence too.

Desada exchanged a glance with Prince Allard. He was stewing as he walked, arms crossed and face red with frustration.

A giggle escaped her and he finally snapped, spinning around swiftly to face their followers.

Desada looked in time to catch Tuboy diving behind a tree and Memet ducking unsuccessfully behind a bush.

"You could at least *pretend* you're not following us!" Prince Allard shouted.

A moment passed and then both of the brothers exposed themselves.

Memet crossed his arms, mimicking Allard's pose.

"Why?" he asked. "Are you going to try to attack us again if we don't?"

"It's not safe to let you go off on your own," Tuboy added.

"So you're just going to follow us the whole way?" Allard demanded.

The twins glanced at one another and shrugged.

"You think Soluc is one of the monsters this land has to offer," Memet said. "That Nemir is in need of being rescued. Just how are you planning to get Nemir away from Soluc, without his consent?"

Desada frowned. She actually hadn't thought of the logistics to that yet.

Prince Allard spluttered, searching for an answer.

Finally, Desada stepped in.

"I have my bow and Allard has his sword."

Memet scowled.

"I hope you're not saying that you're planning on killing my brother," he said dangerously.

Desada swallowed.

"Well, I guess not."

"We'll knock him out," Prince Allard said, helpfully.

"Yes," Desada agreed. "We'll sneak up on him."

Tuboy frowned.

"That doesn't seem fair," he said. "Nemir likes Soluc, I could tell. How do you know he'll leave willingly?"

"Fine! We'll knock them both out!"

Desada shot Prince Allard a look, but he seemed to be serious.

Memet laughed.

"Okay, I like that idea. I'm in," he said.

Allard glared.

"You're not invited," he said.

Desada looked between the brothers and Allard, biting back a smile.

"They're coming anyway, remember?" she asked.

Allard groaned.

***

Nemir sat at the edge of the pool, his feet soaked in the soothing water, all the way up to his calves.

His leg was almost completely healed already. It didn't hurt at all. The wound was still visible, it looked raw and tender, but there was no sign of the infection after the hour he had spent submerged in the warm depths of the pool.

Nemir guessed that within a few days, all he would have left was a thin scar as reminder.

Maybe he would have blanched at the thought of a scar with so much history before, but now he couldn't help but want it there. Soon enough, it would be the only thing to remind him of this wild nightmare. It would be the only proof that it had actually happened.

Once he was home again, Nemir would be able to look at the scar and know that he had survived something incredible. Once he and Soluc were unbound that was.

"He should be waking soon," a voice said.

Nemir started a little and tore his gaze away from Soluc's still form, where it had landed yet again.

Seneca stood silently at the edge of the trees, a soft smile on his lips.

Nemir returned the smile. Seneca and the other elves had saved them just as the life had been slipping from their veins. Nemir wouldn't soon forget the way that everything had suddenly become light and dizzying in those last moments.

The elf walked easily to his side and slid down to sit cross legged next to Nemir by the pool, not making a noise, save for the rustle of his silky robe.

Nemir wore a similar one. After all of the elements directly touching his skin for days, the soft silk felt so smooth and nice.

The elf brushed his pale green hair behind an ear, exposing a point that was nearly identical to Soluc's though it was much smaller.

It was odd. The elves looked simply like the more slender and delicate versions of oves. They were closer to humans in size, with no scars, jewelry, or tattoos adorning their bodies and all the roughness of the oves was completely absent. Their hair, although also worn long and in intricate patterns, was all in various unnatural shades that Nemir had never seen on a living being. Oves had strictly human colors.

Despite all of that however, the resemblance was still there. They were like two halves of the same coin.

"How do you feel?" Seneca asked softly. Caught staring, Nemir blushed but his host didn't seem to notice, much less care, about Nemir's thorough examination of him.

"I'm feeling alright," he said. "Much better than I have since I was captured by the oves at least."

"That's good."

Nemir glanced at Soluc. His head was above the water and a soft leather strap was keeping him submerged in the healing depths, while also holding him up. Even so, Nemir didn't feel safe leaving him alone like that, unconscious, in the water. What if he drowned?

"Thank you for saving us," he said finally.

Seneca chuckled softly.

"You've already said that, twice," he reminded him.

Nemir looked at him.

"I know," he said. "But I really mean it."

The question he'd been burning to ask since they'd arrived, forced him to go on.

"We came to you on purpose," he said, "to ask for your help. We didn't know whether you'd even want to see us."

After a moment's pause, Seneca asked the inevitable question.

"And what help would you like?"

Nemir swallowed.

"We want the bond removed," he said.

Seneca blinked, surprised, and Nemir pushed on.

"We didn't want it. The only reason that it was even done to us was because Soluc's brother wanted an easy way to kill him and—" he shut his eyes, "I really want to go home."

Seneca was looking at him so strangely that Nemir was hard pressed not to keep on babbling, or worse, start barking orders; his instant defense reflex.

He bit his lip and tried to remain silent, though he couldn't stop from shifting uncomfortably.

"I'll arrange a meeting with the priestess for the morning," Seneca said.

Nemir sank in relief. Finally, this was all going to be over.

"Truth be told, we don't often rescue *anyone* from the ogres, unless it's one of ours… but even then, we're hesitant."

Nemir blinked at Seneca's words.

"Why is that?" he asked.

Seneca smiled.

"Any elf foolish enough to fall into an ogres trap, just might *deserve* to be had for dinner."

Nemir's eyes widened.

"Then why did you save us?"

Seneca tilted his head, thinking.

"Well," he said. "There were a variety of reasons. The first of which, being that you clearly weren't in your right minds when you fell into their trap. You were already desperate and injured, that was clear. Now, that wouldn't normally be enough, especially considering that your friend is an oaf but..."

"But what?" Nemir pressed.

"Well, amongst other things, Elves are driven by instinct." He said. "Instinctively, we knew to save you. Maybe because you really needed us, maybe because your lives will really change things for the better, who knows."

Nemir processed this news, his brain sorting through the way they'd unhesitatingly killed two beasts in order to save two strangers. That was all just instinct?

"What do *you* think the reason was?" he finally asked.

Seneca frowned.

"I could *feel* you. Soluc too."

"Feel us?"

"Yes," he said. "I could feel what you felt and that was reason enough to help you."

"Do you regret it now?"

Nemir jumped at the sound of Soluc's voice. He swiveled around, finding the oaf awake, his eyes half open, watching the elf unguardedly.

Seneca didn't seem at all surprised. He simply smiled at Soluc.

"Why would you ask that?" he asked.

"Because I'm an oaf," Soluc answered at once. "My kind is a bastardization of your race. We're worse than those ogres."

"I don't know if that's true," Seneca said. All traces of that soft smile of his were gone.

"It is," Soluc said. "It's getting worse and worse. One day we'll all destroy ourselves and no one will need to do a damn thing." He lifted his head with visible effort, attempting to straighten himself.

Nemir crawled to the edge of the pool behind him to help. He gripped Soluc's shoulders, steadying him as he sat up ad removed the straps.

At the touch, Soluc gripped his hand tightly, more tightly than he intended, Nemir guessed. He looked up at Nemir desperately.

"Then you won't have to deal with any of us again," he whispered.

Nemir's eyes widened as he realized what Soluc meant. That the destruction of his race would be a positive thing for Nemir. That it would be a good thing for everyone.

He shook his head, numbly. It was the healing pool he knew, that was making the oaf so lucid and open, but the look in his eyes told Nemir that he really meant it.

Soluc shut his eyes.

"We have the capability to be something else," he whispered.

He took a shaking breath.

"We're worse than the ogres," he said. "We could have been something better, but we've just given in instead."

"That's not true," Nemir whispered.

Soluc smiled bitterly up at him.

"My own brother wants me dead so badly that he's willing to track us down and kill me himself."

His voice was shaking, his eyes sharpened by a glassy sheen.

A twinge of pain ran through Nemir at that. He was sure that Soluc was feeling it too, but for his own reasons. This time, this was Nemir's own pain.

He had never even considered how much Soluc was hurting from that little fact. He couldn't imagine how it would feel if Desada wanted to hurt him. Let alone Soluc's desire to lead his people to something better. There was a reason that Nemir had been brought into this mess and for the first time, he felt like he was really beginning to understand it. It was true that their people were difficult to understand. They were repulsive and sadistic and filled with what Nemir could only describe as malice.

But one little fact still remained.

"I don't want you to be destroyed," he said.

Nemir slipped his feet back into the pool decisively and directed Soluc's head to gently lie in his lap.

Soluc looked up at him and Nemir tried not to blush. Surprisingly, it wasn't that hard. He didn't care if Soluc wondered about his motives. He wanted the oaf to be comfortable. No, that wasn't quite right. What Nemir wanted, was to comfort him.

He stroked back the long red hair, moving strands from Soluc's face, exposing his defined jaw, high cheekbones, and his large, serious eyes.

His eyes began to flutter shut but after a moment, he stiffened and tried to lift off of Nemir's welcoming legs.

"Your wound," Soluc said simply.

Nemir pulled him back down, sternly.

"It's fine," he said. "Relax."

Nemir looked up, belatedly remembering that Seneca was there, and found that they were completely alone in the dim clearing, the softly lit pool gave the only light. He wondered when the elf had left, but didn't care all that much. The elves here had a way of simply vanishing when they wanted to. Nemir had no clue where they went. He knew there were many of them but the dense forest seemed silent and empty despite the obvious signs of life here, such as this little secluded pool.

Nemir didn't know what it was. Either the atmosphere, or the newly refreshed blood coursing through his body. Maybe it was the calmness he was feeling now, for the first time in days, either way, it was making Soluc look far less intimidating right now.

He hadn't looked *properly* frightening since he had dived at that chimera, but until now, he had always maintained his fierceness, at least.

Running his hands into Soluc's soft, wet hair, the oaf just looked like an over grown and confused man.

He sighed and Soluc's large eyes fluttered open, exposing that deep green that looked so lovely against his dark skin.

"What's wrong?" Soluc asked.

Nemir couldn't help but smile a little bitterly.

"Would you stop being so concerned about me?" he asked. "That's how you ended up like this."

He gestured to the warm pool hugging Soluc's body and went back to his previous task of running his fingers through Soluc's hair.

The oaf reached up, grabbing his hand and stopping him. His eyes fixed on Nemir's. He pulled the hand to his lips, pressing a kiss into his palm.

Nemir shivered.

"It was worth it," Soluc said.

Nemir glued his eyes to the water. He couldn't think of anything to say that would fit in here. In fact, no words would fit, he realized, only actions.

Soluc sighed.

"Why is it?" he asked, when Nemir showed no sign of speaking, "that you're still so scared of me?"

Nemir's eyes widened, his gaze snapping to Soluc's.

"I'm not," he insisted, but the sincerity in his voice was seriously lacking. Soluc gazed at him, hard and then finally, he looked away. Alarmed, Nemir watched as Soluc began to pull away. Nemir forced his hand out to clamp around Soluc's shoulder in an iron grip.

"I'm not!" he insisted, but that wasn't true. "Or—I guess I am, but—"

Soluc was staring at him and Nemir's voice promptly died in his throat.

He took a calming breath, attempting to sort through his thoughts but they were all a jumble now.

"I am afraid of you," he said slowly. That much was true, he knew. "But not for the reasons that you think."

Soluc turned around fully, to face him, resting hands casually on either side of him in a pseudo embrace. Nemir assumed it was supposed to be a calming gesture but it was having the complete opposite effect.

"What do you mean?" Soluc prompted gently.

This was the problem, right here. Whenever Soluc wasn't so close, Nemir felt safe to be with him but when, for an instant, it was too *intimate* then —

"I'm afraid of you getting too close to me."

The composed mask on Soluc's face cracked the slightest bit.

He looked away for a moment but didn't pull back.

"Those times," he said. "I thought you wanted it too. If you don't want me to —"

"No." Nemir was shaking his head. "That's not it at all, I *do* want you to —" He choked a little on the word and swallowed before continuing.

"That's what I'm afraid of. I want you," he admitted. His body was not enjoying this honesty.

His whole face felt flushed, his eyes were stinging. "But I don't at the same time."

He looked at Soluc and quickly away again.

"This whole thing is so wrong," he whispered.

Soluc slipped his hands against Nemir's thighs, gripping him through the silky fabric.

"I don't think it's wrong," he said simply.

He lifted a hand, pushing it into Nemir's hair and pulled him down into a kiss. Nemir complied. He could think of no reason not to.

Their lips met softly and only for a moment, but it sent a shock through his body.

When they parted, Soluc didn't let go; keeping him close, but not moving to do more.

"In the morning," Nemir started, "They're going to reverse this bond for us."

Soluc nodded.

"I know," he said. "But right now, we're still married."

Regret rushed through Nemir. This was their last chance to be together and feel—well, *anything*, for one another.

He leaned forward, suddenly brave from that thought and pressed their lips together once again.

Soluc was frozen in surprise for only an instant but then he pushed himself against the pool wall, closer into Nemir, engulfing him in a strong embrace.

Nemir's arms wrapped around his husband compliantly and then suddenly, he was being lifted into the air.

He opened his eyes, pulling back for a moment as they were sinking together into the warm healing waters.

"Your wounds," he suddenly gasped.

Soluc unlocked his lips from Nemir's jaw long enough to growl, "Forget them."

He latched his lips against Nemir's neck, sucking and flicking his tongue against the skin there and Nemir chose to do as he was told.

His head fell back with a soft moan, his fingers weaving into Soluc's hair, encouragingly.

Soluc pulled away with a curse, fixed a hand on each side of the robe adorning Nemir's body and yanked it in opposite directions.

Nemir's jaw dropped at the ripping.

"Stop that!" he squealed. "It's not mine!"

He struggled to pull it from Soluc's grasp but the oaf shook his hands away.

"If they have a problem with it, they can deal with me."

The fabric tightened against Nemir's wet body while he tore it, his arms and chest flexing.

Nemir didn't even have the strength left to argue. It felt so good to have it desperately ripped off of him. It felt good to be naked. Most of all, it felt good to have Soluc grab him roughly, all previous gentleness forgotten, and squeezed him against his body.

Their lips met in a rush of heat. Suddenly, his back smacked into the wall of the pool and Soluc pinned him against it, his large and straining member pressing hungrily into his thighs.

A shiver of pleasure coursed through him, shooting between his legs. Suddenly, Nemir understood Soluc's frustration. Soluc's clothes were in the way. Of all people, why was *Soluc* wearing clothing in the first place?

He reached down, tugging at the red silk. When it wouldn't loosen, he shoved his hand into the thick, wet fabric, finding what it wanted at once.

Nemir wrapped his fingers around him, marveling at his size. That had been inside of him. He moaned and then realized rather belatedly that Soluc had stilled.

His hot lips were no longer nipping and licking at Nemir's neck, his large hands no longer running heatedly over his body.

Nemir froze. Was something wrong?

Nemir's stillness seemed to remind Soluc to move. He took a soft, shuddering breath against his neck.

"Don't stop," he gasped.

With a start, Nemir realized what Soluc meant. He began to pump his hand. This was the first time he'd touched Soluc and the shiver that ran through his large body, sent a thrill through Nemir.

Why hadn't he done this sooner?

Soluc lifted slightly, pressing his forehead against Nemir's.

The heated look in his eyes only intensified as their eyes met and it spread into Nemir like a wild fire. He couldn't remember ever being so aroused. Each stroke over Soluc sent a pulse through him as though he could feel the pleasure that he was giving.

Soluc's eyes fluttered shut, his lashes brushing Nemir as his breath quickened.

Soft puffs blew against Nemir through trembling lips. He leaned up, brushing his own against them briefly and sending a shock into his member which was straining for attention.

He didn't care.

Pleasuring Soluc felt a lot better than anything he'd experienced before. The thought made his fist clench enthusiastically around him and suddenly Soluc's fingers gripped into his arms.

His hips jerked into Nemir's hand and with a cry he strained against him, hot liquid spilling against Nemir, slightly hotter than the water and warm enough to make Nemir wish he could feel it again.

He collapsed against Nemir, breathing heavily into his neck, kissing it softly as Nemir pulled his hands from their task. He wove those fingers into Soluc's long hair, relishing the tremble those little kisses were sending through him.

He felt so powerful right now. Even though Soluc was probably eight feet tall and with the muscles of a warrior, Nemir could bring him to his knees if he wanted to and Soluc would let him.

Just as Nemir began to sink into the comfort of Soluc's large, content embrace, those large arms wrapped around him, suddenly lifting him into the air again.

"What are you doing?" he asked, but that was rather unnecessary as he was promptly seated on the edge of the pool, Soluc in between his wet legs.

He fell silent, remembering the last time that Soluc had lowered himself over him like that. His mouth went abruptly dry, eliminating any words he could have said.

Soluc's soft lips touched his tip, kissing it as thoroughly as he did Nemir's mouth.

Nemir's eyes, glued to the sight. Within seconds he was gasping. He had already been nearing the end just from the look in Soluc's eyes while he had stroked him.

The look in his eyes now was even harder to watch without bursting. As those expert, delicious, *amazing* lips closed around him Nemir's eyes rolled shut, his head falling back in pleasure. One swift movement of his hot tongue and Nemir cried out, unable to hold on any longer.

Soluc stayed around him. Sucking like he had the last time, until every last tremor had run through Nemir's ecstatic body.

Finally, Nemir found the strength to lift his head and look at his lover. Soluc was climbing from the pool. He pulled the unraveled clothes from his body and came to lie next to Nemir.

They didn't speak as he pulled Nemir close, settling his head on his arm so that their faces were close.

Nemir slid his hand into Soluc's hair once again, he was beginning to believe that it belonged there, and pulled him close into a languid kiss.

Their lips didn't part for a few minutes and when they did, Nemir snuggled against his husband, letting sleep pull him down.

He was exhausted still, from the past few days and especially from the emotions whirling through him.

Tomorrow his life would go back to normal and somehow, he'd find a way to be ashamed of the pleasure he'd taken from tonight's actions. Right now though, he could care less.

CHAPTER SIXTEEN

Soluc squeezed Nemir's hand gently in his own. Something about this whole situation was incredibly backwards.

"And you see, my people would never accept their prince being married to another species, and they definitely would not accept my marriage to a male, even if he *was* human," Nemir was saying.

He shot a glance at Soluc uneasily.

"If we don't get this reversed, then I'll lose everything that I have."

Soluc tried not to smash his face into the nearest tree and just barely succeeded, although the effort gifted him with a splitting headache.

They were sitting on the soft grass, clasping each other's hands in the morning light, and facing the small congregation of elves that had come to hear them out.

"We completely understand your dilemma," Yana said. They had been brought before the stunning, white-haired elf to plead their cases. She was clearly the leader in affairs such as these. Several others watched, but altogether, it was still a private affair.

"We have had our own elves forced to mingle with ogres and even oves in the past and the situation has always been difficult."

She turned her milky gaze to fix on Soluc.

"And what of you?" she asked. "What are your reasons for wanting this bond reversed?"

Soluc blanked.

He supposed he should have known that he would be consulted too, after all, he was one half of this forced union.

"Well... it was done without my consent," he said.

That should suffice.

Nemir threw him a pleased look and Soluc wanted to bash his head against something again.

Why was this so damn confusing?

He'd felt so complete lying with Nemir in his arms all night long. Every doubt in his mind had faded, every trouble had disappeared. Even his wounds were mostly healed. Granted, he supposed, it was because of the enchanted water that he'd spent so long laying in. But in his opinion, it never would have worked as well without Nemir by his side the whole time.

Nemir had opened up to him on a level he never thought was possible and it made the rest of Soluc's life seem suddenly and inexplicably unimportant. Somehow, he was sure that everything before last night had just been leading up to those moments.

This morning, he'd opened his eyes to find those gorgeous black orbs gazing at him contentedly, a soft smile on those pink lips. He'd wanted to burry himself into Nemir and find a way to live in him.

Then, right when he'd been about to suggest that he do just that, Nemir had smiled and said, "let's go find Seneca and have our bond reversed."

Nemir squeezed his hand gently, and Soluc reached up promptly to squeeze the bridge of his nose.

Again his hand was squeezed, more tightly this time.

He looked down and found Nemir staring at him expectantly with raised brows. Soluc frowned.

"What?" he asked blankly.

Yana cleared her throat.

"I said, is that your only reason for wanting this bond reversed?" she asked.

Soluc felt himself flush slightly, a very uncharacteristic response. Maybe Nemir was rubbing off on him.

He cleared his throat uncomfortably.

"Sorry, I just had a brain fart for a second there." He laughed awkwardly and stopped immediately when everyone else remained silent.

Nemir's jaw dropped, his eyes wide, staring at him like he was an actual idiot.

Soluc swallowed.

"I—I want to get this bond reversed because…"

Wait—did he have any reason at all, to want this bond reversed?

As far as he was concerned, Nemir was probably the best person he could ever be married to. Only, Nemir wasn't an oaf, and Soluc wasn't any part human. If their roles were reversed, he supposed that marrying an oaf would probably be a major step down for him.

Soluc had nothing to lose by being with Nemir. In fact, with him, he got everything that he wanted or needed; the warmth, the companionship and more. But Nemir lost everything.

He lost his whole life and for what? For Soluc.

That hardly seemed like a worthwhile trade.

He swallowed.

"I want Nemir to be sent back home," he said finally. "I want him to have his family and friends. I want him to go back to the life that he had, before I came in and wrecked it."

Soluc could feel Nemir's eyes on him, watching him intently, but couldn't bring himself to meet his gaze, keeping them fixed on Yana instead.

She watched him closely, her gaze seeming to reach into Soluc effortlessly and read everything in him. It took all his might to not look away.

Finally, she dropped her gaze to Nemir, and smiled at him kindly.

"I understand your reasons well," she said. "Your life may never be the same as it was before you two were joined together, and you," she fixed her gaze kindly on Soluc, all previous intensity gone. "What a noble reason to give up your sacred bond. You represent your kind very well."

She smiled briefly, and offered out her hand. One of the other elves helped her to her feet.

"Unfortunately, I cannot reverse a bond when both parties do not unanimously *want* the bond reversed."

Stunned, Soluc stared as she easily turned to go.

"What?"

Suddenly, Nemir was on his feet.

"But you have to!" he said urgently.

She paused and turned to look at Nemir over one shoulder.

"I do not *have* to do anything for you," she said pointedly. "In fact, we've already done too much."

"But—"

Soluc gripped Nemir's hand, stopping him. The other elves closed around Yana, blocking her retreat, and maybe they didn't look like the most hostile of beings, but there was no mistaking the finality of their gestures. Soluc wasn't eager to be on the receiving end of those bows.

"We aren't welcome here much longer," he said.

It seemed they had overstayed their welcome, especially by demanding more services. Frankly, Soluc was surprised that it hadn't happened sooner.

"Let's get our stuff and go."

Trembling, Nemir looked up at him.

"And what stuff is that?" he asked. "Half torn animal skins that still smell like pig meat?"

Soluc grimaced.

"Fine," he said. "We'll leave them."

He grabbed Nemir by the hand to pull him away, but it was yanked free the second Soluc's fingers closed over him.

"Don't touch me," Nemir hissed softly.

Soluc swallowed. When he could think of nothing to say, he simply turned and walked away, hoping desperately that Nemir wasn't too angry to follow.

After a few heart stopping steps, he heard Nemir come after him, shuffling as he did.

Edges from the end of the elves' land, Seneca stepped out from the trees before them, stopping them.

"Came to see us off?" Soluc asked.

He smiled softly.

"I heard about the hearing," he said. "Yana rarely reverses a bond. I wouldn't worry."

"That's easy for you to say," Nemir muttered.

Soluc held back a response.

Instead, he came forward until he was standing just before Nemir.

"Have a safe journey home," he said.

"I don't know if I'm going back anymore," Nemir said. All anger seemed to fade away, leaving only the note of remorse in his voice.

"I'm sure you will," he replied easily.

He looked back at Soluc.

"You have a safe journey as well," he said.

Soluc nodded.

"Thank you," he said.

Seneca turned back to Nemir, brandishing a shining silver blade from his robes. It looked plain but smooth and strong.

"I noticed that you might need some protection of your own," he said. He pushed the weapon into Nemir's hands. "Keep this close, just in case."

Soluc bit his tongue, trying to remain silent while they watched Seneca disappear into the trees. Finally, he grabbed Nemir's hand again to lead him away.

This time Nemir didn't pull out of Soluc's grasp, distracted by the weapon clutched in his grip.

"What does he think you'll need that for?" Soluc growled.

Nemir snickered.

"You maybe," he retorted.

Oh, so he was only snappy with Soluc, it seemed.

Nemir wasn't about to stab him with a blade unless he was suicidal, but the remark still stung just as it was meant to.

"Oh yes, because I'm so prone to attacking you."

"No," Nemir said at once. "Although," he amended, "you *did* have me kidnapped, and beaten and—"

"You know none of that was my fault!" Soluc snapped, turning on him. "All I've done is keep you alive since the moment we met!"

"That's not enough!" Nemir shouted, yanking his hand free.

"What do you want from me?" Soluc demanded.

"I want you to *want* the bond reversed!"

Nemir's voice echoed through the forest around them, making them both fall silent.

"You've kept me from being hurt physically," he said, tears springing into his eyes. "But this hurts more."

Soluc's frustration promptly slipped away, no matter how much he wanted to hold onto it. He dropped to his knees before Nemir, tilting his chin to look at him through his tears.

"I meant everything I said back there," he whispered fiercely. "I don't know why she wouldn't do it."

Nemir furiously blinked the tears away, shaking his head.

"I know you did," he said.

He pushed into Soluc's arms, squeezing him until he could barely breathe. Soluc just held him back.

He knew what he was feeling was wrong, but the happiness coursing through him would not go away.

He could feel Nemir's heartbroken-heart pounding against his and his own felt a similar pain for him, but it was mixed with the strongest joy he had ever felt.

They would be together. They would always be together. Even if no one else in the world approved, it didn't matter because they would have each other.

Suddenly, Nemir gasped and pulled back. He looked down slowly at his side where a little white feather was stuck in his arm.

Soluc's eyes widened.

He knew that kind of feather and he knew that technique. Looking back up at him in dazed confusion, Nemir's eyes widened just as something hard struck the back of Soluc's head.

Why did he keep letting these things happen? Soluc wondered, as everything went dark around him.

CHAPTER SEVENTEEN

M emet laughed, watching as Desada whooped loudly. She clapped hands with Allard and then looped around to do the same to him and Tuboy.

"Congratulations boys," she said grinning. "I believe our plan was a complete success."

Allard laughed.

"Even the oaf didn't realize we were coming." He winked at Desada. "I think you would make an excellent addition to my personal royal hunting party, if you ever chose to join me."

She frowned.

"But I thought you only hunt alone?" she asked.

He nodded.

"Yes well, one more person couldn't hurt. And you two," he turned to Tuboy and Memet with a grudging smile. "If you ever come near the human kingdom, let me know."

Tuboy smiled but Memet simply rolled his eyes.

"Sure thing," he said and then without warning, he reached out and ruffled the prince's hair, coming up to Desada next, he bent down low and placed a kiss to her soft cheek.

After that, Tuboy pulled her into a tight embrace so that she all but disappeared and then, despite Prince Allard's protests, did the same to him.

The wannabe-macho prince struggled for a moment and then grudgingly patted Tuboy's back in return.

"Right, let's get out of here before Soluc wakes up," Memet said. He glanced down at the crumpled lump of their brothers. "It shouldn't be too long now."

With Tuboy's help, they untangled the lovers' limbs and dragged them apart so that they were lying on their backs.

After quickly checking him over, Nemir was easily hoisted onto Allard's shoulder like prized game. That done, Tuboy and Memet came to their still brother, and unceremoniously they each grabbed an end of him.

Memet hated sticky goodbyes and so he simply turned and began to lead Tuboy away. He could feel his twin looking back at the other two, could feel their eyes on him as well and with an inexplicable twinge, he carried on.

In retrospect, he was glad that they had captured the wrong prince. Allard would have put up too much of a fight—meaning he would have been dead in no time. And worse, he would have had no one to come looking for him.

This though had already turned out perfectly. Nemir was safely being carried away with Allard and Desada and whenever Lenroy *finally* caught them, he would be up against the three of them. The idiot needed a smack of reality. No way was he killing their brother. Memet was confident that once he was being held down, he would be easily convinced.

They were headed back in the direction of their camp. He knew that they would still be where they'd been left. Ilaj was in charge and no one would dare go against his words, unless they wanted him to punish them personally for it.

"You hit him too hard," Tuboy suddenly said.

Memet glanced down at the lifeless feet in his hands and shrugged.

"The longer that he's unconscious, the farther away from Nemir we can get."

He sighed. Perhaps it was rather cruel to tug his big brother away from his lover like this, but it definitely seemed like the most fun way to do it at least.

Several more minutes passed and finally, Memet began to feel his twin's worry.

"Why is he still out cold?" he asked.

Tuboy frowned at him.

"I don't know," he said. The touch of fear was evident in his voice.

"Put him down," he instructed, his heart skipping unpleasantly.

Tuboy complied at once, kneeling down as Memet placed Soluc's legs onto the ground so that his head wouldn't bump any more than it already had.

He crawled over Soluc's body, all the way up to the chest and lay his head down gently against his brother's chest. To his relief, his heart was beating steadily against Memet's ear, and with each breath, Memet's head rose and fell with Soluc's rhythm.

"He's fine," he said, meeting Tuboy's anxious gaze.

Memet's words did little to alleviate the worried expression on Tuboy's face.

He sat back with a sigh and reached out, stroking back Tuboy's hair comfortingly.

"Would you like to camp here until he wakes up?" he asked.

Tuboy nodded mutely.

Tuboy helped him carry Soluc to a flatter area. They moved only a short distance away, but the spot was much better to set him out in and build a fire.

Tuboy took guard at Soluc's side while Memet set to work. He was completely silent, and unfortunately his emotions always caught Memet like wildfire. He was starting to really worry. He couldn't let it show, but—

"Why isn't he awake yet?" he demanded.

He turned away from the 'fire' which was still a small pile of barely smoldering sticks and dropped down next to both of them.

He placed a hand on Soluc's forehead, feeling for fever, but he felt normal.

Tuboy took his hand, gripping it tightly, comfortingly.

"Don't worry," he said. "By the time the fires built I'm sure he'll be up."

Memet scowled.

Typical. Memet was only worried because Tuboy was so worried and now Tuboy was the one offering him comfort.

The world was an unfair place.

He sighed and turned back to his previous task, hoping his twin was right.

After a couple of silent minutes, Tuboy sighed and lay down next to Soluc, stroking back his hair.

"Do you think Nemir is awake yet?" he asked.

Memet shook his head, mutely.

The poison in those darts put an oaf out for an hour, at least. On someone Nemir's size, it would be much longer. Maybe two or even three hours.

The fire was up and roaring and Soluc still didn't stir.

They rolled him a little closer to the fire to keep him warm, and wrapped his strange elf clothes closer around his body.

Memet tapped his fingers against Soluc's arm absently.

He would wait one more hour exactly. If Soluc didn't return to consciousness by then...

"Mmm."

Memet sat up, his heart skipping and they both leaned over anxiously.

"Soluc?" they asked together.

Soluc's eyes fluttered open slowly, fixing on his brothers. He blinked blurrily up at them.

"Memet?" he asked. "Tuboy?"

"How do you feel?" Tuboy asked.

"You've been out for almost two hours."

His brows frowned but the hint of a smile touched his lips.

"Am I dreaming? Or hallucinating?"

He asked, as though those were the only two options available to choose from.

"Neither," Tuboy laughed. "You're here with us now."

Soluc's smile brightened.

"Where are we?" he asked. "Is Nemir okay?"

His voice was heavy and slurred, almost like he had been drugged.

They glanced at one another.

"We're nearing the eastern side of the swamp, heading back to the camp."

"But Lenroy—"

"He won't touch you while there are three of us to go up against. Don't worry. Now that the panic has died down, we can go back to the camp and sort everyone out."

"We'll get everything back to normal in no time," Tuboy added.

Soluc frowned.

"Where's Nemir?" he asked.

He reached out a hand as though expecting to find him there, close enough to touch.

"He's safe now," Tuboy assured him.

"Safe?"

Soluc blinked, the last of the haze disappearing from his eyes and suddenly he shot up, his eyes scanning their little area.

"Where's Nemir?" he demanded.

Tuboy placed a soothing hand on Soluc's arm.

"He's with his sister and the other prince."

Soluc blanked, his eyes raking his brother's faces like they were speaking gibberish.

"His sister?" he asked. "What prince?"

"You know," Tuboy said. He glanced at Memet, clearly concerned about his brother's mental wellbeing. "The human one. The one we were supposed to capture in the first place."

Soluc stared, his jaw slowly dropping as all color drained from his face.

"You left him alone with two humans?" he asked slowly.

***

Nemir blinked the last vestiges of sleep from his eyes, and realized that he was staring at a bum.

"Ahhhh!" he struggled against his captor, swinging out wildly until his fist smacked into a head and he was dropped unceremoniously onto the ground.

"Ow! What in the name of—"

"Nemir! You're awake!"

Nemir shot into a sitting position so fast that his head spun.

"Desada!"

This was not good. He was dreaming while he was awake now. Clearly his body couldn't handle the stress of the lifestyle that he had been leading over the past few days.

Suddenly, his little sister sprang into his arms so hard that it winded him. After a painfully long moment, Nemir had an inkling that this was not a dream. She was real. The pine like scent of her hair and the feel of her in his arms could not be mistaken for anything other than his sister.

And she was wearing pants and a shirt. Clothes! Something that he had barely seen since he'd arrived on this god forsaken land.

It was so refreshing. It was like he could almost *taste* home.

He looked up through his tears and found another unexpected sight.

"Prince Allard," he said, stunned. Clearly this was the owner of the bum that he'd gotten such a close look at.

"Hello," Prince Allard said with a grin. "Sorry for letting you get kidnapped."

Nemir shook his head numbly.

"You did nothing to apologize for," he said.

"Actually he did something to be *thanked* for," Desada said. She pulled back to look up at Allard affectionately. "He helped me rescue you."

They'd rescued him?

It felt strange to think of the two of them as his saviors because, well, that job fell to someone else.

"Where's Soluc?" he asked.

"Who cares?" Desada laughed.

She jumped to her feet, and offered a hand to Nemir to help him up.

He ignored it.

"Where is he?" he repeated.

Allard leaned over, placing a comforting hand on his shoulder.

"Don't worry," he said. "He's miles away by now, on the way back to his camp."

Nemir stared, the words slowly sinking into his mind.

"He left me?" he asked uncertainly. That didn't sound like Soluc. He wouldn't just leave Nemir unconscious and without even a goodbye. Nemir *knew* he wouldn't, but the thought was already sending tears springing to his eyes.

Desada and Allard exchanged an uneasy glance.

"Well, he didn't exactly leave. He was carried away by his brothers. He was unconscious."

Nemir gasped.

"His brothers?" he demanded. "Which brothers?"

Catching their mistake at once, Desada shook her head fervently.

"No, not Lenroy," she said at once. "The twins Memet and Tuboy."

She grinned at his shocked expression.

"How do you know them?" he asked slowly.

Getting comfortable, Desada dropped to her knees before her brother and invited Allard to take a seat next to her.

He did with considerably more grace and listened, interjecting where ever he could about the journey they had taken to get Nemir back.

As they drew to an end, the sick feeling in the pit of Nemir's stomach thickened.

"Our job is to get you out of the forest and home as quickly as possible, while the others take care of the situation."

Nemir didn't speak. Nothing logical was coming to mind. Nothing that either Desada or Allard would understand.

"We—um, we heard about how the ogre forced himself on you."

Nemir was confused for a moment and then suddenly understood.

"He's not an ogre," he said. "He's an oaf."

He pushed himself to his feet, trying to get away from their sympathetic eyes.

He knew that the twins wouldn't have said it like that, which meant that it was only the two of them assuming that Nemir had been forced. Of course. Why would he *willingly* make love to a beast of another species?

"Nemir..." Desada started uneasily. "Why are you so distressed? We just rescued you."

She looked confused and desperately upset. Clearly this wasn't the reaction she had expected. He shook his head, attempting to clear his thoughts.

"I know you did," he said. "I'm not upset, I just—"

Oh lord, now he was lying too.

"I didn't say goodbye," he realized.

Why? Why did this hurt so much? He had wanted to separate himself from Soluc permanently only hours ago and now…

"I didn't tell him," Nemir realized. "I didn't tell him that he didn't wreck my life."

He really couldn't stop the tears now. He shoved his face into his hands. The severity of the thought almost made him turn and run back, screaming Soluc's name.

He turned on his heels.

"Nemir!"

He was grabbed by the shoulders, spun around and shaken.

"Stop this," Allard said fiercely. "We have to get out of this forest. From here, we can make it out by nightfall and then it's an easy and quick trek to the palace. We'll be there, in civilized society, in no time at all."

Nemir supposed that this was supposed to be some sort of a comfort but the little pep talk failed miserably.

Civilized society. The one place in the world that Soluc would never fit into, would never even be *allowed* to fit into. The one place that he might never come to get Nemir back from.

He blinked.

Was that what he wanted? To live in the wilds with Soluc for the rest of his life?

He lifted his head heavily and looked into Allard's eyes. The prince looked beyond confused and Desada, standing by his side, looked downright alarmed.

Nemir swallowed hard.

"You're right," he finally said.

Relief passed over both of their faces.

Not giving him time to change his mind, Prince Allard smiled.

"Let's get going then, shall we?"

Nemir nodded but began to walk only when Desada took his arm in hers and tugged him.

"I hope mom and dad aren't too angry that they missed my wedding," Nemir said absently.

Both of them stopped and looked at Nemir slowly.

CHAPTER EIGHTEEN

"They're humans!" Soluc bellowed. "They can't defend themselves! They don't know *how* to handle the forest!"

Another, even more terrible thought occurred.

"Oh god. They're going to starve to death."

His brothers were laughing now, although Tuboy was trying valiantly to hold it back by biting his lips.

"I don't think you understand the severity of the situation," Soluc grit out. "They're like *this* big!"

He held up a hand to his chest and both of his brothers burst into laughter, ignoring his feelings.

With a groan, Soluc dipped his head, massaging the bridge of his nose with his thumb and forefinger. That was one thing that spending so much time with Nemir had done for him. He was feeling less inclined to jump forward and rip their pretty braids off of their damn heads.

Memet began to choke on his laughter.

Okay, maybe just one braid…

Tuboy stepped between them, his hands raised in surrender, but the grin was still plastered on his face.

"They're safe," he said. "They're hours from being free of the forest and Allard and Desada are quite the little hunters. If anything attacks them, they'll defend your little man."

Soluc crossed his arms, ignoring Memet's continued snickers, and completely aware that now he was sulking.

He didn't want the other two to be good at protecting Nemir. That was *his* job, dammit.

With a huff, he turned and stalked to the edge of the clearing, pressing his forehead into the rough bark of a tree.

"Why did you drug us again?" he asked.

"We didn't drug you Soluc," Memet said. "We just bashed you over the head—hence your brain damage."

"I know, you dick, but you drugged Nemir, and therefore me."

"What are you talking about?" Memet asked. "We really did hit you too hard, didn't we?"

Soluc turned a death glare on the two.

"You drugged Nemir and I felt it until the first symptoms passed. That's the way these kinds of bonds work, or were you not there with dad when our mother had her leg amputated?"

It was cruel he knew, to bring up their parents' deaths, but the words shocked them both into silence.

"You're not saying…"

"Yes," Soluc answered. "Lenroy had me bound to the boy in secret. They wanted to kill us both."

Tuboy's eyes darkened immeasurably and for once, the fierceness in both of the twins' eyes matched. He looked capable of anything, just like Memet.

"That's too far," he whispered.

With a sigh, all of the anger faded from Soluc's body. This was what Nemir had wanted anyway. In the end, they *could* always manage living apart.

Even if it sucked.

"It's okay," he said. "As long as Lenroy comes after me, and as long as I know Nemir is alright, then it's okay."

His brothers didn't seem convinced.

"Is it really okay?" Tuboy asked. "Living apart from your bond partner won't be easy."

Nemir's little speech in front of the elves shot into Soluc's mind and he swallowed.

"I can handle it," he said.

They frowned, glancing at one another.

"I don't think that's the problem," Memet said stepping forward. "We didn't think that there was any danger in separating you."

Soluc stared.

"Oh come on," Memet said. "I know we don't think too highly of our dear brother right now, but he's not *that* stupid. Wouldn't *you* go after the easier target?"

Soluc cursed.

Memet was right. Soluc's feet started moving before he even knew which direction he was going.

"Wait! Soluc, we don't even know for sure that he's following them! We haven't caught wind of him since you went the wrong way around the swamp!"

Soluc didn't stop, didn't even slow down. This wasn't just any helpless human that they were talking about. This was *his* helpless human.

How could he let them take Nemir so far away from him? How, when he knew the boy was always getting into trouble on his own.

Memet and Tuboy were suddenly at his side, tugging him to stop.

"As romantic as it is running off after your partner through the forest, everything from a mile around is going to hear you coming."

Soluc moved to yank his arms free and then realized that it was true.

If he wanted to catch up with Nemir, then yes running was probably the best thing to do, but if he wanted to catch up to Lenroy—and then throttle him to within a minute of his life, then maybe he should do it with a little more stealth.

The rage boiling within him, told him that the 'throttling' was an incredibly good idea…

"Calm now?" Tuboy asked.

Soluc nodded mutely.

They began their walk, tracing their steps until they came back to the edge of the elf territory. It was funny how, the moment they stepped out of bounds, the elves didn't give a rat's ass about what happened to them. It made Soluc seriously wonder about the fact that they had rescued a human and an oaf in the first place.

Deciding to simply thank their luck, Soluc walked to the spot, examining the area closely. He could see the slight imprints from where he had lain and then clearly been dragged from. Nemir's prints were there in the soft grass too, but were much harder to see. He was so light, it was no wonder.

Soluc could pick him up as though he was nothing. He shut his eyes at the onslaught of memories from the hot pool; lifting Nemir into the air and letting his small frame drag down his body as he slid into the water.

He tried to blink the image away, only partially succeeding.

"Here," Memet suddenly said.

He was kneeling before a small patch of mud, barely visible against the up-sticking roots of a tree.

"That could be from anything," Soluc said.

Memet shook his head. Rubbing the tip of his finger into the half dried stuff, he lifted it to his nostril, taking a quick sniff.

"It's from the swamp," he said. "Sniff for yourself."

He offered his finger to Soluc, but Soluc pushed it away.

"I'll take your word for it."

"None of us went through the swamp," Tuboy said unnecessarily.

It didn't take long to find more of the greenish brown gunk. Soluc found it by stepping in it. The elves had given him a lovely pair of sandals and the sound of it sloshing against the leather was hard to ignore.

"Over here," he called.

His brothers joined him with a grimace.

"This is the way they carried Nemir off."

"I can see that," Soluc said. "They didn't even try to hide their tracks."

"None of us bothered," Memet retorted. "We were carrying heavy loads."

Soluc frowned.

"Nemir's not heavy," he informed him.

They began their walk in silence, following the little traces of Lenroy that they found along the way; the scrape of a blade across a tree trunk, a large footprint in soft earth.

Some of them just seemed careless, but Soluc knew his brother often *was* exactly that. The fact that he'd managed to formulate such an intricate plan to dispose of them was beyond impressive, too bad that he had failed to carry it out properly. Soluc's stomach squirmed uneasily at the thought of lying dead with Nemir in a field somewhere, while Lenroy took up his post as leader.

Then again, there was likely no one who would have disputed it. They might not have even cared. If anything, the fact that Lenroy was cold blooded enough to murder his own brother would probably have earned him respect. Except from the twins, of course. Even Ilaj would have respected it, despite not being so happy about it.

Soluc did let him get away with more than anyone else would.

Soluc couldn't help it, he liked the twisted creature.

"Is Ilaj in charge, back at the camp?" he asked.

"Yes. You should have seen the look in his eyes when he took charge."

"I was afraid to leave," Tuboy admitted.

Soluc chuckled.

"Lenroy would never have that much authority over them."

"Neither would you."

Soluc shot his brother a glare.

"There."

Tuboy pointed to yet another sign of Lenroy's passing.

"It's almost too easy to track him," he said leaning on the broken branch. "It's like he wants to be caught or something."

"Keep walking," Soluc said. "We're almost out of the forest."

Tuboy followed the order and they continued on in relative silence. The trees were thinning here.

Soluc noticed, as he always did, that at this edge of the forest, the air smelled different. It smelled like the ocean. They were so close to it, that even the air smelled like that fresh salt. He had only been to the water's edge once, but the memory was unforgettable for someone like him, who got his water from cold streams and melting snow.

"This doesn't seem right," Memet suddenly muttered. "Hasn't it been a while since we saw anything?"

Soluc and Tuboy looked around as one. The thinned trees were undisturbed.

"So, he was careful here."

Memet shook his head.

"No," he said. "It's easier to leave trails here. The earth is softer, and it's lighter."

Soluc frowned. It was true.

Something was wrong.

"Maybe he got them?" he asked, voicing his thoughts. But no. If he had, then why was Soluc still alive?

He took several steps forward, searching for signs of some passage. Slightly to the left of their chosen path, he found the trail of decidedly human feet moving forward.

"Nemir was here," he said. "They've left the forest."

But Lenroy hadn't. The thought sent a flutter of relief through him.

"Then where—?" Tuboy started.

Soluc continued to stare down at the little footprints. They were undeniably cute. After a long moment, a soft, choking noise finally made Soluc and Memet spin at the sound. They both froze.

Lenroy stood before them, looking ragged and worn. He had a steel blade pressed closely to Tuboy's neck, his arms around him in an otherwise pseudo hug.

"Hello brothers," Lenroy said coldly.

"If either of you move, I'll kill him on the spot," he said.

"Lenroy, please—" Memet started.

Lenroy cut him off by pushing the knife into Tuboy's flesh, drawing blood.

Tuboy gasped.

The sight of the blood slipping along the blade made Soluc's entire body suddenly shake.

"It's me you want," he started. "I'll come to you."

Nemir flashed into Soluc's head and he swallowed. He couldn't let Nemir die, but Tuboy...

Tuboy let out a soft moan of pain and Soluc took a step forward.

"Don't! Do you *want* him to die?" Lenroy demanded.

The desperation was so clear in his voice that Soluc's entire chest twisted in pain. Lenroy didn't want to do this. Soluc *knew* that he didn't.

"Don't kill him, please," Memet begged.

His equally desperate voice sent tears springing to Lenroy's eyes.

"I don't want to," he said. "I don't even want to kill *you*."

He spat the words at Soluc, but the importance of them weren't lost on him.

"Then stop now," he whispered. "It's not too late."

"It *is* too late!" Lenroy shouted. "I've put too much into this. It's too late to stop now."

"You want me dead?" he asked. "Fine, just let Tuboy go and I'll let you do whatever you want to me."

"No," Tuboy whispered, but there was no need, because Lenroy was shaking his head furiously.

"I have a better idea," he hissed.

His blade dropped from Tuboy's neck and before even a breath of relief could be taken, he struck Tuboy's back, hard.

The sound of the blade slicing through flesh could be heard, even where Soluc stood, feet away.

"No!"

Memet was at his twin's side before his body even dropped to the ground and Lenroy was gone, running.

For a split second, all Soluc could think of was going after the bastard and making him feel his pain, and then the thought cleared and his little brothers were on the ground, one shouting incomprehensively, while the other bled all over the ground.

"Tuboy," he dropped down, beside him.

"I'm okay," he muttered weakly.

Soluc shook his head and pried him out of Memet's arms, taking the calm role.

He flipped him over and saw, to his immense relief that Lenroy hadn't struck him in the spine. The wound lay on the very side of his lower back, just by the hip.

"It might just be a flesh would," he said. Having nothing else, he ripped some of the fabric free off his robe and held it tightly around his brother.

Tuboy hissed in pain and Memet mirrored the sound, out of sympathy. Soluc doubted that he did it on purpose, but still, he wondered if the twins felt each other's pain in the same way that he felt Nemir's. It might not be a magical connection, but it was strong and fierce, just the same.

"How does it feel?" he asked.

Tuboy only stared, mutely. He was losing too much blood.

"The elves," Soluc whispered, realization dawning on him. He turned to Memet. "We'll take him to the elves. They can heal him there. They won't turn him away if he's like this. I know they won't. They're not as bad as they pretend to be."

He looked up to find Memet staring at him, his eyes wide and filled with tears.

"What about you?" he asked, shaking.

"I'll carry him," Soluc said. "I'm stronger than you."

Memet shook his head.

"Lenroy went after Nemir. This was his way of distracting us."

A chill ran through Soluc's body. It seemed that they were experts in underestimating their brother.

"Well it worked, didn't it?"

He knelt before Tuboy. His eyes were drifting shut and Soluc gripped him by the chin, forcing their eyes to meet.

"Stay awake," he ordered. When Tuboy didn't respond, he shook him gently. "Did you hear me?"

Tuboy nodded.

"Yes," he murmured. "Awake."

Soluc slid his arm under Tuboy's knees but Memet gripped him, stopping him.

"We don't have much time," Soluc whispered to him desperately.

The words sent more tears shooting into Memet's clear green eyes.

"But Nemir—"

"Forget Nemir!" Soluc finally shouted. "He doesn't *want* me!"

The sting of the words hit Soluc, coupled with the shock of Tuboy's injury. He tried to blink the pain away but it wouldn't go.

"You said the others could take care of him, didn't you?" he demanded.

Memet squeezed his arm tightly.

"What if they can't?" he asked. "You're my brother too, Soluc."

Soluc shut his eyes, feeling Memet's urgency. If he died along with Tuboy…

"I'll go," he said.

He lifted Tuboy carefully into Memet's arms.

"If you hurry, it won't take long to get there," he said. "Tell them that you're my brother and that I'll find some way to repay them." He gripped Memet's shoulder. "Beg them if you have to."

He stroked Tuboy's hair back from his face. He was sweating.

"Remember to stay awake," he said gently.

Tuboy only nodded.

Kissing them each on the cheek, Soluc sent them on their way, watching them go for only a minute while he cleared his thoughts.

Lenroy wasn't far ahead of him. He was fast, but Soluc was faster. If the little ones could

only hold him off for a little while, then Soluc
would take care of the rest.

CHAPTER NINETEEN

N emir rubbed the back of his neck for the third time.

He risked a glance at Desada and Allard. They both appeared more than a little mystified by Nemir's behavior, but aside from that, nothing seemed to be amiss.

"You really don't feel that?" he asked.

They shot each other an uneasy glance.

"No Nemir," Desada finally said. "Are you sure that you don't want to sit down for a little while?"

He sighed.

"Look," he said. "I'm not crazy. It's called intuition. You know people always say that you should trust your instincts, and the one time—."

"Okay, okay fine, you have a bad feeling, we believe you."

Allard stared at them with his brow raised until Desada shot him a scathing look and he nodded in agreement.

"Yes, something bad is going to happen," he agreed.

Nemir scowled.

"Fine, don't believe me," he huffed. "But if I drop dead suddenly then it's both of your faults."

This time Allard laughed.

"And why, pray-tell, would a healthy young man just drop dead?"

"Because if Soluc dies, then I will too, obviously," he retorted.

They both fell silent and stopped walking. Nemir continued on without a beat.

Not so funny now, is it? He thought haughtily.

"Wait." Allard grabbed him by the arm, stopping him. "Nemir, is that true?"

His serious expression made Nemir pause.

"Yes," he said. "We feel each other and if he gets hurt, I'll feel it right away."

A distant shouting filled the air. As one, the three of them looked toward the trees as the sound died away with a soft echo.

"I know that voice," Nemir whispered, a chill traveling over him.

"Me too," Allard said.

270 | The Oaf Prince

"It's not Soluc," he said. "I would know if he was hurt."

"It's one of the others," Desada whispered.

Suddenly, she was close to Nemir's side, pulling on his arm.

"Let's go," she said. "Please, I have a bad feeling."

Oh *now* she cared about feelings.

They broke out of the forest only minutes later, the bright sun striking down at them without shade or cover. Nemir felt he could cry from joy. For the first time, this second kidnapping seemed like the blessing that it truly was.

He squeezed his eyes shut, feeling the sun's heat warm his face and kiss his eye lids. He half-wished that he never had to see another tree again.

Nemir's mind shot fiercely to Suvahl and he missed it with a sudden ferocity.

"Nemir." Desada tugged on his sleeve. "Come on."

Together, they turned toward the palace but Prince Allard stopped them.

"If we're being followed, we should just get to safety as fast as we can."

He took off straight forward and Nemir and Desada didn't hesitate in following him.

The ocean was visible first, and then a harbor town came into sight. The houses were few and far between but the market was large. The wharf stretched along the water with boats docked all along. There were people everywhere.

Nemir didn't know who saw what first, but eyes seemed to be drawn to them. He supposed they made an odd sight, the prince of Tasnia practically running from the forest accompanied by a woman in men's clothes and a man dressed like an elf. Either way, as they reached the town, people were staring.

And then the screaming started.

Nemir turned, despite himself, stumbling at the sight. Lenroy, massive and wild, running toward them at breakneck speed. He looked ferocious. He looked ready for blood.

A thrill of fear ran through Nemir and it froze him in his tracks.

People were running all around him, taking cover, and hiding. All the people here were fishermen and farmers, he didn't expect them to stop and fight, but still, he wished they would.

Alone, one human could never defeat an oaf with brute strength.

He knew that as he watched the prince walk fearlessly toward Lenroy.

Prince Allard drew his sword, the ocean wind whipping his hair dramatically to the side as his blade caught a glare of sun. For once the drama was well deserved and Prince Allard really was the stunning, strong knight that he always acted like he was.

He marched to Lenroy, his footsteps never pausing or hesitating as he walked the wharf.

"Nemir!" Desada shouted. "He's doing this for you! So you can get away!"

She pulled on his sleeve, trying to force him on, but Nemir's feet were stuck to the ground.

He shook his head fervently.

Sword or no sword, Prince Allard couldn't defeat Lenroy. He was sacrificing himself for nothing.

Suddenly, Nemir's feet found their ground and he was running toward them.

"No!" Desada shouted, but it didn't matter because Allard was almost on the brute.

"Allard!" he shouted.

If the prince heard him, he pretended not to. His blade swung through the air in a perfect arc.

Stunned, Nemir watched blood spray from the tip of the blade as it scraped Lenroy's arm.

With a shocked cry, Lenroy swung out. Allard tried to block it. He nearly succeeded, but Lenroy swung swiftly with his other arm, smashing his fist sickeningly across Allard's skull and sending him flying sideways onto a lower dock, blood splattering all around him.

"No!"

Nemir wasn't thinking. Clearly he wasn't, because Allard was a much better swordsman than he was. He was stronger, manlier and altogether smarter when it came to things like fighting, but Nemir still ran toward Lenroy, like he had a chance to save his friend.

Nemir pulled the ornate dagger from his belt without thinking, the carved vines cutting into his palm, and he intended to use it.

Suddenly, he was shoved roughly aside and Desada was passing him.

No. What was she doing?

"What do you want with my brother?"

She spoke like she was threatening, but she wasn't, she was begging.

Lenroy took a step toward her, the glint in his eyes visible from here.

"Desada!"

Fear rushed Nemir and he dove for the two of them, but it didn't matter. Lenroy shot out his hand, his long fingers gripped around Desada's delicate neck.

"No!" He lunged at Lenroy's arm, clamping around it.

With a frustrated growl, the brute flung Desada aside and replaced his grip on Nemir's neck instead.

Nemir was sure that his head would be squeezed from his body. He struggled futilely against the iron hold, blood pounding behind his eyes.

And then he remembered the dagger.

His arm swung up wildly and suddenly he was dropped unceremoniously to the ground.

He looked up at Lenroy, gasping through the tears and spots to see what he'd hit.

Blood soaked the oaf's arm as it swung forward, striking Nemir across the jaw with an angry shout.

Nemir's knife flew through the air, landing with a clunk behind Lenroy.

For a moment, they both stared at it and then Lenroy looked back at him, a slow grin crossing his face.

***

The wind whipped Soluc's hair into disarray as he ran, it caught on twigs and branches until he was out of the woods, exposed in broad daylight in the open Tasnian fields.

It took only a moment to realize that he didn't know which way they had gone. There was no one in sight and the high grass whipping in the ocean breeze worked too well to obscure their tracks.

To the left was the palace; straight ahead was one of the port towns. Soluc had only ever been to the right where the ocean dipped low enough that he'd had to look down on it from secluded cliffs.

At the very least, he knew that they wouldn't have run for the cliffs. Taking that way led away from all civilization until you reached the mountains and then of course, the rest of the oves. So yeah, no civilization.

If they headed for the palace and the capitol, there was no way that they would make it there on time. Lenroy would be on them like bees on honey.

Squeezing his eyes shut, Soluc blindly followed his gut, rushing straight ahead toward the nearest town. He hoped desperately that they were there, otherwise the town people might not be very happy to have him. More than that though, it was the only way that the humans had a chance.

He drew on the town quickly, rising above the horizon slowly as he ran up hill, until all he saw before him were buildings and water and ships. An entire fleet of ships, large and unlike any he'd ever seen, was headed directly for them. They were painted all black with enormous sails the color of sea foam to direct them.

The buildings were small, well maintained shanties and sheds, a market and one or two caverns and brothels awaited sailors, but as Soluc drew near, he realized how amiss the whole place looked.

From a distance, he always saw hundreds milling about the place but now, it was entirely deserted.

Seagulls cawed above him as his feet stepped onto the planks leading toward the water. For a while, his footsteps were the only sound beyond the ocean and the wind and then he heard a cry.

Nemir.

Soluc took one step forward, and suddenly he couldn't breathe. He collapsed to his knees, hands grasping ghost fingers around his neck.

Nemir was dying. He would never see him again.

Soluc knew he had promised to do this for his brother's sake, but it wasn't just for Memet that he was here. He wanted to see Nemir. It was selfish, he knew, but it was all he wanted and now they were both going to die and neither of their wishes would come true.

He pressed his forehead to the planks below him as blood rushed painfully behind his eyes.

Nemir would never get home and Soluc would never see him again. It wasn't fair.

Soluc gasped for air and suddenly, it came. With a rush of oxygen, he collapsed back onto the ground, his eyes burning, his lungs screaming for more.

After a prolonged moment, Soluc realized the obvious. He wasn't dead.

Which meant that Nemir wasn't either.

Soluc pushed to his feet and ran, his heavy steps stumbling and echoing off the wood. It was a wonder that they didn't hear him coming but when he turned the corner, he found Nemir lying in a heap on the planks, looking up at Lenroy. His face was a mask of fear and disappointment.

"Nemir!" Soluc shouted. No sooner had the words left his mouth, then did Soluc realize his mistake.

As one, they both looked at him. Nemir's eyes widened in shock but Lenroy didn't seem surprised.

He jumped forward, seizing Nemir by the collar of his robe and lifting him as though he was weightless. He crushed Soluc's lover to his chest, his hand gripping Nemir's chin.

Soluc knew that grip. Any neck would snap when held like that. All it took was an extra little *twist*.

"No!" Soluc shouted. "Please don't hurt him!"

He was still gasping for air and he could see from here that Nemir was too.

Please don't let these be our last breaths.

Suddenly, tears were pouring unabashedly from Nemir's eyes. A familiar rage filled Soluc at the sight. He would kill his brother for making Nemir cry.

But if he charged at him from here, then they would both be dead before a step had been taken.

"It was me," Nemir suddenly gasped. He choked a little but didn't look away from Soluc. His eyes were glued to his, so securely, that Soluc knew nothing could break that gaze. Not even death.

"I was the one," he said. "I was the one who didn't want the bond removed."

If anything could have shocked Soluc that was it. The anger faded, the fear disappeared. For a moment, all that was left was the sudden euphoria that surged through him.

"Nemir," he whispered. It was all he could say.

"Enough!" Lenroy shouted.

He tightened his grip on Nemir and Soluc felt the strength with which his hand clamped around him.

"Do you think this is a joke?" he demanded.

"I'll leave!" Soluc suddenly shouted. He couldn't remember ever begging in his whole life, but it was coming out of his mouth without an effort. "I won't come back. You can tell everyone I'm dead!"

Lenroy shook his head furiously.

"I can't!" he shouted desperately.

"Why?"

If Lenroy wanted to do this so badly, why hadn't he already?

With a sudden clarity, Soluc understood.

He took a step toward his brother, slowly, non-threateningly. Lenroy flinched, but didn't move otherwise.

"You have to die," he whispered fiercely. "It's the only way."

"For what?" Soluc asked.

He took another step.

"For any recognition at all!" Lenroy suddenly shouted. "You wouldn't understand Soluc!"

Maybe not, but he understood that his brother couldn't watch him die. He couldn't kill him, just like he couldn't kill Tuboy.

"Try me," he said.

Soluc took another step, and suddenly a sharp pain ran through his foot.

Nemir shouted out as Lenroy stepped down on his toes.

"Don't take another step," Lenroy said to Soluc with a grin. "It looks like you don't think I'm serious."

He glanced down at Nemir briefly and then back up at Soluc, his eyes set, the smile gone.

"Goodbye, big brother."

"No!"

Soluc leaped before Lenroy moved, smashing into him and for once, ignoring Nemir entirely. The pain was doubled for him, as he felt Nemir's pain from the impact, but he ignored it, landing atop them both with a crash.

Lenroy's head hit the ground hard, but without so much as a pause, his fist swung out, cracking Soluc across the jaw.

He flew backwards, landing with a thud. Somehow, he had enough presence of mind to grab the human by his robe and yank him out of the way.

"Run!" he shouted, as Lenroy landed atop him heavily. His fists pounded ceaselessly into Soluc's face. He shouted, throwing up his legs and sending the other oaf flying over his shoulders.

Soluc climbed unsteadily to his feet, turning to his brother just as he leapt onto him again.

His teeth dug into Soluc's shoulder painfully. He let out a cry, swinging as hard as he could into his brother's stomach, but Lenroy stopped him.

He gripped his forearms with those damn sharpened nails, digging them in deep and drawing blood at once.

Shouting, Soluc broke away, stumbling back onto the hard ground.

Lenroy pounced on him, ignoring Soluc's strikes as though he was too numb to feel them. He held him down with his knees and gripped Soluc by the hair, attempting to hold him still as his other hand shot out like a knife into his chest.

All five of his nails dug into Soluc's flesh and next his fingers pressed deep into him. He could feel his flesh ripping around those strong fingers, knew what was happening, even though he had never had his flesh torn apart by bare hands before.

Soluc screamed and something dug into his hip. He gripped it, not realizing what it was, until it sliced his hand.

Blinded by pain, he thrust it up. It stuck into flesh, but nothing stopped. The hand was still pushing into him, he was still held immobile and then suddenly, Lenroy went limp, sagging against him.

Dazed, Soluc stared up at the clear sky above for a moment and then shoved his brother off of him.

Lenroy was still alive, the blade buried deep under his ribs and his hand soaked in Soluc's blood.

Numbly, Soluc looked down at himself and found his chest drenched with blood and still pouring.

A hand gripped his arm and he looked down at Lenroy. He was pretty certain that only your own life was supposed to flash before your eyes in times like these, but all he could see was Lenroy.

They had been glued together as children, always fighting but also building hideaways and sneaking off on hunts when they weren't allowed.

Somehow, the years in between then and now weren't there in Soluc's memory and all he could see was that he had killed his little brother.

Lenroy watched him mutely, his hand digging into Soluc's arm, his eyes boring into Soluc's eyes and then they simply drifted shut.

For some time Soluc sat there, unmoving, staring at his brother and then two small arms wrapped around him from the back, squeezing him tightly.

Suddenly, Soluc came back to life.

He took a long breath, closing his eyes against the sight of his brother and turned into Nemir's welcoming arms. Two other humans stood behind Nemir now, but Soluc barely even registered them.

"Are you okay?" Soluc asked against his chest.

Nemir nodded, his head resting against Soluc's.

"Are you?" he asked.

Soluc didn't know how to answer that.

"I killed him," he finally said.

Nemir nodded again.

"You had to," he said.

He pressed a soft kiss to Soluc's head and despite his size, helped him to his feet. Soluc was too shaken to find it funny.

Nemir led him away, onto the top of a grassy hill. From here, Soluc couldn't see his brother lying dead where he'd left him. He had no doubt that Nemir had led him there on purpose.

He was torn between running back and staying beside the still form and burying himself in Nemir's arms. Thankfully, Nemir made the decision for him, and tugged him down into a strong embrace.

Tears burned Soluc's eyes. His fingers dug into the fabric surrounding his lover and it was strangely comforting to be able to grab onto him so fiercely without worrying about hurting him.

Nemir simply let him cry and when he finally pulled away, he looked almost as sad as Soluc felt.

"I guess it's all over now," Nemir said.

"Everything?" Soluc couldn't help but ask.

"No."

The fierceness of Nemir's response was strangely gratifying.

"Not us," he said.

"Where are the others?" Soluc finally thought to ask.

"They got pretty big bumps to their heads, but they're okay. They're waiting for the ships to dock."

Reminded suddenly of those strange ships, Soluc looked out at the dock. Several were already pulled in. The town's people were timidly emerging from their shelters, shooting frightened and uneasy glances in Soluc's direction.

Ignoring them, Soluc watched the people coming off of the ships.

"What are they?"

Nemir leaned in to him, linking their arms as they watched.

"They're Suvahl warships," he said easily.

Soluc blinked.

"What?"

"See that one there?" Nemir asked, pointing. "I think I just saw my father come off of it."

Soluc's jaw dropped.

"What? Where?" he demanded.

Ignoring him, Nemir reached up, tilting Soluc's head down to look at him.

"This isn't going to go over well," he said softly. "Do you mind if we forget about it for the two minutes it will take for him to talk to my sister and come up here?"

Soluc wordlessly wrapped his arms around Nemir, leaning down to press his face into his soft curls.

Nemir's arms came around him and Soluc felt much like he had just that morning, waking up content in Nemir's embrace. Everything washed away while they stood there.

"Does your chest hurt?" Nemir asked.

Soluc shrugged.

"I've felt worse."

Listening to Nemir explain why he didn't want to be married to him had been a heck of a lot worse in fact. But now…

"You really didn't want the bond to break?" he asked. It was foolish to want so much confirmation, but he couldn't help it.

Nemir's arms tightened around him.

"No," he said. "I just thought I did, I guess. I thought it would be easier."

Despite everything, a smile touched Soluc's lips. He opened his eyes and caught sight of a human man walking toward him. He had hair as dark as Nemir's, but it was relatively straight. He could see the dark eyes from here though, and clearly saw the resemblance, despite the lines of worry and age on the older man's face.

Soluc shut his eyes, pressing his face against Nemir again, anxiety bubbling within him, and squeezed him closer.

"Kiss me," he suddenly whispered.

Nemir lifted his head, twisting it to see how close his old man was but Soluc gripped him by the chin, pulling him into a kiss.

His lips. He would never get over how soft and sweet Nemir's lips were. He could kiss them for days on end and never get tired of it.

"Ahem."

Nemir pulled back so abruptly that Soluc blinked a moment, wondering what had happened, before realizing where Nemir had gone.

He risked looking at Nemir's father, the impeccably dressed King of Suvahl and swallowed.

He had never been concerned about first impressions before but this was undoubtedly the worst one he'd ever made.

The king raked his eyes over Soluc, his eyes lingering on the blood soaking him and by proximity, also soaking his son.

"Nemir," he said. "We came as soon as we heard of your kidnapping."

Nemir smiled, tears filling his eyes.

"Father," he whispered. "I'm so happy to see you!"

He flung himself into his father's arms, instantly crying and to Soluc's shock the King began to shed tears as well.

"Stop," he sniffled. "I can't let the rest see me crying."

Nemir tried to pull away obediently, but his father pulled him back into another embrace.

"You're okay?" he asked finally, pulling back.

Nemir nodded.

"Yes," he said wiping his eyes. He reached back blindly, until his fingers found Soluc's hand and gripped it tightly.

"I had people watching out for me the whole time."

His father caught the action but didn't say anything.

"Desada told me," he said. "And Prince Allard as well. You were lucky to have them there for you. We all were."

Nemir shot Soluc an uneasy glance.

"They weren't the only ones watching out for me," he said.

He tugged Soluc forward so that they were standing next to one another. Soluc tried not to shift awkwardly, but it was hard under the scrutinizing glare.

"This is Soluc," Nemir said uneasily. "He's the leader of—some of the oves and he—he's saved me more times than I can count."

At that, his father's eyes finally softened as they looked up at Soluc.

"That's why he's like this." Nemir gestured to his chest and Soluc shrugged awkwardly.

Finally, the king smiled.

"For that," he said. "I own you my thanks. I couldn't live without my children, no matter how much trouble they are."

Soluc found himself smiling back at the kind expression.

"It was my pleasure," he said.

"Come." He pulled their hands apart and walked in between them, linking with both of their arms.

"We need to get you medical attention, at once. Luckily for you, my personal doctor has accompanied us and should be somewhere near."

Confused, Soluc exchanged a glance with Nemir. Didn't he imply that his father would be completely against this?

"So…" Nemir glanced at his father. "You're okay with this?"

"With what?" his father asked absently.

Nemir swallowed.

"With our Marriage."

All softness left the king's expression at once.

"There's no marriage here that I know about," he answered.

Nemir looked at Soluc, his eyes wide.

"We were forced to marry by the other oves, father. Didn't Desada—"

"It doesn't count unless I say it does," he growled.

Soluc frowned.

"Actually—"

"Ah, here he is."

He gripped a freckled man by the arm and pushed him toward Soluc.

"Heal him," he ordered.

He took Nemir by the arm, pulling him away.

"Hey!"

Nemir spun to look at him.

"I'll come find you after!" he shouted.

Stunned, Soluc watched as Nemir was ushered away.

He looked around the milling crowd. Everyone was staring up at him. They were trying to act unimpressed, he could tell, but were failing miserably. He watched as two people walked straight into one another, their eyes glued to Soluc's large form. Oves didn't *ever* venture into human territory, and Soluc wanted nothing more than to be away from all these humans and back in the shelter of the woods.

"Are you coming?"

He glanced down at the medic. He seemed unperturbed by Soluc's towering height, but the blood on the other hand, was making him turn a distinct green color.

"Are you sure you're a doctor?" he asked.

The man shot him a scathing look.

"Of course I am," he retorted.

He led the way back onto one of the ships. Soluc followed uneasily. He had never been on one before and the gentle swaying motion was dizzying at best.

They walked below deck, down a swaying staircase and Soluc felt distinctly like he was in the belly of a sea monster. Finally, they entered a small room. It had in it a small bed, a table and a chair and that was it.

Soluc couldn't imagine staying in it for any longer than a couple of minutes.

The man pulled open his pack and began to sort through the items there.

Finally, he pulled out a small bottle, soaking a cloth in its liquid and without warning, he pressed it against Soluc's chest.

He hissed in pain and instinctively, shoved the man away.

With a cold look, the medic looked up at him.

"Do you want this healed or not?" he demanded.

Sullenly, Soluc allowed the man to continue his ministrations.

It hurt almost as much as when he had gotten the wounds, but he bit his lip and remained as still as he could, while he was cleaned and stitched up.

Where was Nemir? Hadn't it been forever already?

There was a soft knock on the door as the man cut the last bit of string.

"Come in," he called.

Soluc couldn't hide his disappointment when a girl entered the room.

She smiled at him hesitantly and Soluc's heart sped up a little, despite himself. She had Nemir's smile.

"You're Nemir's sister," he said.

She nodded and looked at the doctor.

"Can we have some privacy?" she asked.

He nodded and left.

"Where's Nemir?" Soluc asked.

Her eyes darkened.

"He's being taken back to the palace."

Soluc stared.

"We're going to stay there for a couple of days to sort everything out. My dad's pretty angry that Nemir was allowed to be kidnapped in this country."

"How long will you stay?" he asked her, numbly.

Desada shook her head.

"We're leaving before the week is out."

She looked up at him. Clearly she wanted to say more, but it wasn't necessary.

He wouldn't see Nemir again. Not if they could help it.

CHAPTER TWENTY

Soluc looked out over the construction with a smile on his face. Lately, all he'd done was frown and glower, but today he couldn't keep the smile away. He knew the gesture made by the Tasnian's was more to appease the Suvahl royal family, than to give Soluc a reward for his efforts to save Nemir. But still, it was finally happening. They were getting their own town. Their own land. They counted for more than a nuisance in this country. They were more than just something to be feared.

"You're scaring me."

He glanced over at Memet and raised a brow.

"Why?" he asked. "I'm not throwing things for the first time in two months."

A smile slinked over Memet's face.

"That's what's scaring me."

Soluc rolled his eyes.

"How's Tuboy?" he asked.

This time Memet rolled his eyes.

"It's been two months," he said. "He's probably out climbing trees and hunting."

Soluc frowned.

"He shouldn't be doing either of those things."

Memet sighed.

"Well he's probably not, but even if he did, it wouldn't matter."

He wrapped his arms around his brother pressing their cheeks together.

"He's fine," he said. "Stop worrying."

Soluc rested an arm around Memet's shoulders silently and continued to watch the slow progression of the building.

"What's going to go there?" Memet finally asked, pointing.

"A school."

He got an odd look at this, and sighed. He was getting sick of constantly getting those looks.

"Only five oves can read that I know of," he reminded his brother, "and that includes the two of us."

"Yeah, yeah."

They fell silent once more, until Ilaj slinked up next to him on the other side.

"I want some," he said to Memet, shoving his arms aside and replacing them with his own.

Memet glared at him.

"He's *my* brother," he said. "Get your own."

"No thanks, I have Soluc already."

Soluc rolled his eyes and shook them both away. They just loved annoying him.

"Is anyone giving you trouble?" he asked.

Ilaj shook his head with a sigh.

"Ever since I was in charge of the camp, everyone's been perfectly obedient."

"I wonder why," Soluc muttered.

He'd heard enough stories to be glad that Ilaj was on his side.

"So no hitches with the building?"

Ilaj sighed and exchanged a glance with Memet.

"You're obsessing again," he said.

Soluc glowered.

"Well what else do you want me to do?"

"When's the next time you're going to the ocean?" Memet asked easily.

Soluc stared out over the oves, hard at work, the sound of hammering and shouting fading away.

"I'm not going," he finally said.

He'd been there six times already. He knew Nemir wasn't coming back. He hadn't been allowed to see him, even in the days when he had remained on this land and Nemir hadn't come to see him, even though they'd been so close.

Soluc had waited. He had watched the ships leave, missing even a glimpse of the dark haired human. Until now, he had still been waiting. But enough was enough.

As though on cue, a sharp pain stung his arm. He looked down, assuming that Memet had pinched him, but he was standing completely innocently at his side.

Soluc was confused–and then his heart skipped painfully against his ribs.

It was Nemir.

His heart wouldn't slow down. He could still feel him, even though they were so far apart. They were still connected.

"Pinch me," he suddenly said.

Both Memet and Ilaj were staring at him as though he'd gone crazy but Ilaj reached out and pinched his bicep. He squeezed harder than necessary, but Soluc didn't care.

He waited with baited breath and then after a painfully long pause, a sharp pain shot through his big toe.

"Ah!" He stumbled and then caught himself, looking back at the two with a laugh.

"It's Nemir!" he informed them.

"What's Nemir?" Memet asked slowly.

"Ow!" Another pain ran through Soluc's foot and he kicked a large rock in repayment, laughing hysterically.

Now they *really* thought he was crazy but Soluc didn't care. Nemir was thinking about him. He wanted Soluc to feel him. He shut his eyes as inexplicable tears stung at his eyes.

Okay, maybe he would wait a little longer.

He whacked his hand against a tree, grinning when another pinch stung his arm.

***

Nemir couldn't stop laughing—and crying—at the same time.

A pain shot through his knuckles and he gasped before pinching his own arm and bursting into more hysterical giggles.

Desada, who had stood by the edge of his bed in confusion until now, backed away slowly before spinning and running from the room.

"Nemir's finally lost it!" she shouted down the corridor. "Dad, I'm blaming you!"

Her words made him laugh even harder before he buried his face into his pillows and proceeded to cry.

It had been two months and though he managed to come to dinners now and show his face in public and pretend that he was fine, he didn't think he could do it for much longer.

He missed Soluc with a ferocity that he hadn't expected. He missed holding him and snuggling him and talking to him and running about the forest half naked.

The thought made him notice, yet again, the way that the band of his pajamas dug into his waist. He hadn't really paid attention before, but now that he was here back in 'civilized' society, all he could notice was that they wore so many *clothes*. Layers and layers of it and at every hour of the day and night. And no matter how comfortable it was, it was *never* comfortable enough.

He wiggled around until they lay on him straight and realized that Eliseo was standing over him with a bemused smile.

"Having issues this morning?" he asked.

Nemir blushed and scrubbed the tears from his eyes.

"Sort of," he said.

He sat up and sniffled the last of his tears away before looking up at his manservant.

"Your father and mother would like to see you before breakfast," Eliseo said.

Nemir frowned.

He would never deny how much he loved his parents, but he still did not want to see or talk to them ever again.

"Do I have to?" he asked.

Eliseo sighed and very uncharacteristically, took a seat next to Nemir on his bed.

"Your parents only care for you," he said. "They don't think that being married to an oaf is a very good idea. Can you blame them?"

"Yes," Nemir answered truthfully.

Eliseo ruffled his hair.

"Come now, how are they supposed to let their dear son live in a society they know nothing about, all the way across the sea?"

Nemir shrugged futilely. He was losing the argument, he knew, but that didn't make it any less painful.

"We could visit each other," he said weakly.

A small pain shot through Nemir's upper arm and the tears began again.

Eliseo waited for him to stop crying and then walked him to his parent's chambers.

Nemir pinched himself a couple times as he went. He couldn't help it. He didn't want Soluc to forget him. Not even for a moment.

He knocked on their door before entering alone and stood uneasily by the entrance, wishing he wasn't there.

His mother and father both sat at the breakfast table, overlooking the lush gardens outside and sipping their porridge with round silver spoons. They glanced at him grimly upon his entrance but continued to eat.

Confused, Nemir simply walked to them, pulling out the extra chair at the table and joining them.

He realized his mother was trying not to cry, only as he settled in the seat next to her.

"Mother," he asked slowly. "What's wrong?"

She shook her head mutely, wiping at her grey eyes and finally put down her spoon.

"Honey, tell him," she finally said.

Nemir turned to his father apprehensively. Something bad had happened. If Desada hadn't tried to force him from bed only a few minutes ago, his first thought would be that she was hurt.

His father turned fully in his seat, facing his only son. He looked so serious that Nemir shifted uncomfortably.

"What is it?" he asked.

"Our country hasn't been on very good terms with Tasnia since your kidnapping," he said slowly. "We need to send someone back as an ambassador and as someone to strengthen our ties with the kingdom and their people."

He waited for Nemir to respond. When he said nothing, his father placed a hand over his and leaned forward meaningfully.

"Nemir, we decided that it will be you."

His mother sniffed sadly, but smiled at him.

Stunned, Nemir stared between the two. He was going back?

"You'll have to visit often," his mother said. "Don't you *dare* forget about us just because you're married now."

"We'll be there to arrange for your wedding. You never had a proper ceremony, so King Jareth already said that he would help to arrange one for you. Your ogre may not be royalty, but he's Tasnian and he's *their* damn responsibility in my opinion so—"

"Wait!" Nemir stared at them a little longer. "What?"

His father sighed.

"Nemir," he said. "You've been walking about the palace like the dead since we got here. We thought you would move on but…"

He exchanged a glance with his wife and she leaned forward grabbing his hand tightly in her own.

"We just want what's best for you," she said. "And if this is it, then we'll just have to deal with it."

A pain shot through Nemir's knee. He gasped and they both stared at him.

He couldn't explain through his tears though and so let it pass, pushing out of his seat to embrace them each.

"Thank you," he whispered.

***

Soluc stood on a hill high over the ocean, watching the ship approach. His heart was skidding into his chest so hard that he thought it might break through.

He had been standing here watching for what felt like forever and his nerves still wouldn't stop twisting inside him.

Yes, he told himself. That is a Suvahl ship. Yes, it's almost here. Yes, Nemir is on it.

The thought made his breath hitch, yet again.

Eventually, *finally*, the ship pulled in.

After what felt like forever, people began to disembark.

Soluc's feet were fused to the ground. He couldn't move and only watched in stillness, his eyes raking each person to step on shore.

Finally a young man, with lovely windswept curls, stepped down. He wore all white, practically gleaming in the sunlight. Soluc was suddenly glad to have taken the time to force Tuboy to braid his hair. The intricate style had taken forever to twist around Soluc's head but he was glad to have done it. Nemir had never seen him at his best. Now, he wanted him to *only* see that side of him.

Those lovely black eyes scanned the land desperately with every step Nemir took, and then finally, they rested on Soluc.

Soluc's feet suddenly remembered how to move and he was walking forward, his eyes glued to Nemir's.

They didn't blink or look away until they were standing together, facing one another.

Suddenly, Soluc didn't know what to say. All that he'd known until now, was how much he wanted Nemir back here. He hadn't thought of much beyond that.

"I missed you," he blurted.

With a laugh, Nemir flung himself into Soluc's arms.

The need to think disappeared as Soluc lifted him, instinct taking over. He squeezed his prince as though they could fuse together. Their lips met in a rush, filling each other, tasting each other and Soluc never wanted to let go.

And judging by the way that Nemir's hands gripped into his shoulders, he was never going to let him.

Well, it looks like you made it through the book!
We hope that you enjoyed the ride!

For more fantasy and sci-fi reads like these, please
join our mailing list found at DjinnPublishing.com

About the Author;

Sienna Sway is a Canadian writer. She shares a house with three Irish men, four Spanish brothers, a pit bull and a mystery mutt. Seriously. It's like Full House. One day soon, she hopes to own her own home with her boyfriend and dogs and live happily, with her friends visiting often, family always near and sunshine and waves at her front step.

Until then, Sienna finds her escape in writing about love, passion, adventure and romance.

To get to know her, follow her on;

Twitter- @siennasway
Blog- siennasway.wordpress.com
Goodreads-
https://www.goodreads.com/author/show/5348491.Sienna_Sway
Facebook- facebook.com/siennasway

To read more of her writing;

www.amazon.com/author/siennasway